D0349766

NOODLEHEADS FORTRESS OF DOOM

by Tedd Arnold
Martha Hamilton
and Mitch Weiss

illustrated by Tedd Arnold

HOLIDAY HOUSE  NEW YORK

To the young reader who finished
our first few Noodlehead books
and asked if there were any more.
This one's for you, Calvin!
—Tedd, Martha, and Mitch

Text copyright © 2019 by Tedd Arnold, Martha Hamilton, and Mitch Weiss
Illustrations copyright © 2019 by Tedd Arnold
All Rights Reserved
HOLIDAY HOUSE is registered in the U.S. Patent and Trademark Office.
Printed and bound in May 2019 at Toppan Leefung, DongGuan City, China.
The artwork was rendered digitally using Photoshop software.
www.holidayhouse.com
First Edition
1 3 5 7 9 10 8 6 4 2

Library of Congress Cataloging-in-Publication Data

Names: Arnold, Tedd, author, illustrator. | Hamilton, Martha, author. |
Weiss, Mitch, 1951– author.
Title: Noodleheads Fortress of Doom / by Tedd Arnold, Martha Hamilton, and
Mitch Weiss ; illustrated by Tedd Arnold.
Other titles: Fortress of Doom
Description: First edition. | New York : Holiday House, [2019] | Series:
Noodleheads ; 4 | Summary: Using knowledge from a library book, brothers
Mac and Mac build a fortress but Meatball, armed with a book of his own,
wants to take it from them.
Identifiers: LCCN 2019006111 | ISBN 9780823440016 (hardback)
Subjects: | CYAC: Fools and jesters—Fiction. | Books and reading—Fiction. |
Building—Fiction. | Brothers—Fiction. | Humorous stories. | BISAC:
JUVENILE FICTION / Readers / Intermediate.
Classification: LCC PZ7.A7379 Nrm 2019 | DDC [E]—dc23
LC record available at https://lccn.loc.gov/2019006111

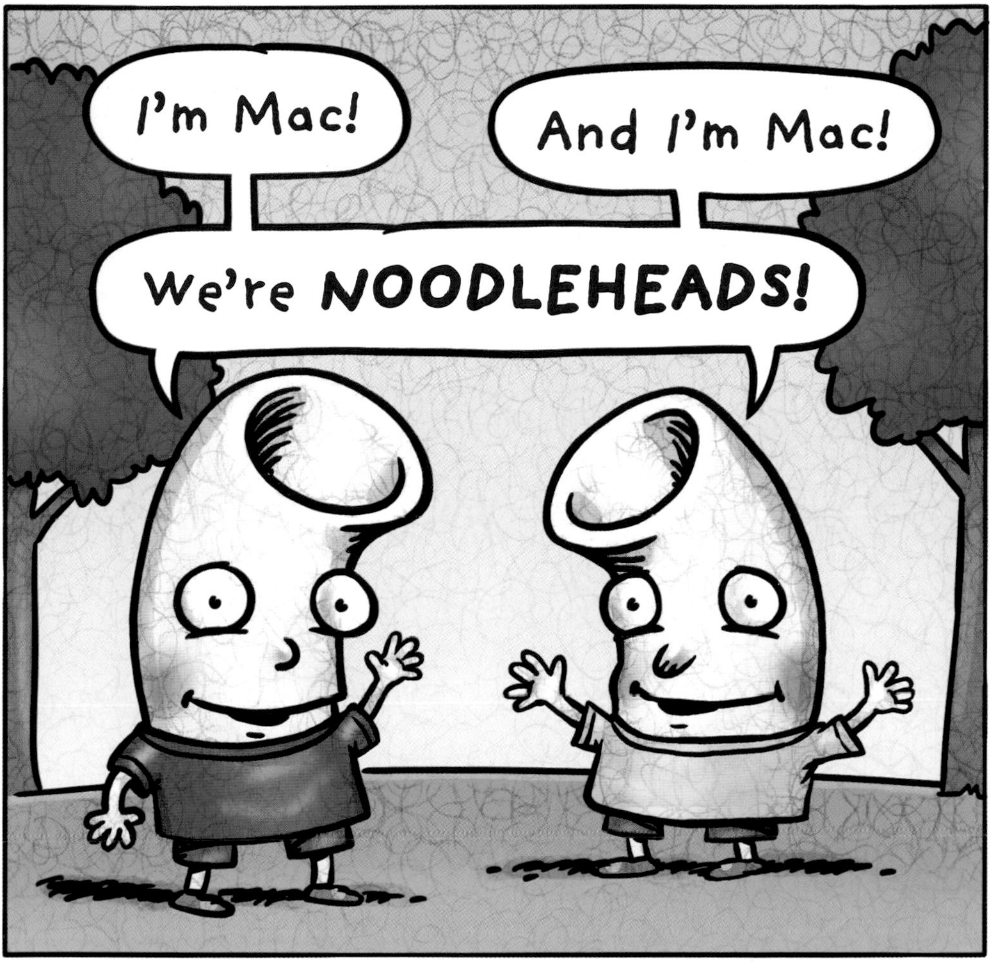
I'm Mac!
And I'm Mac!
We're **NOODLEHEADS!**

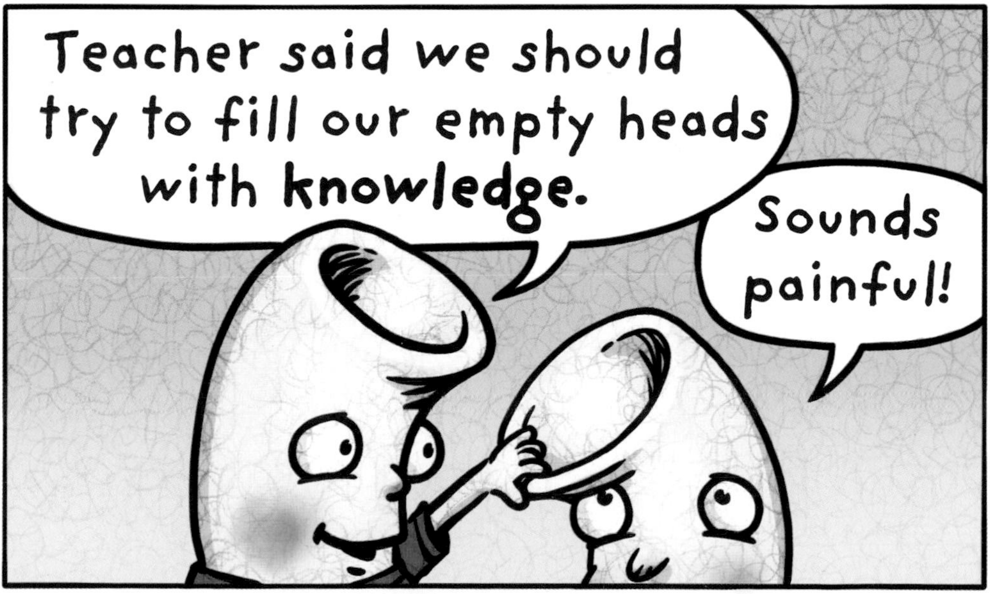
Teacher said we should try to fill our empty heads with **knowledge.**
Sounds painful!

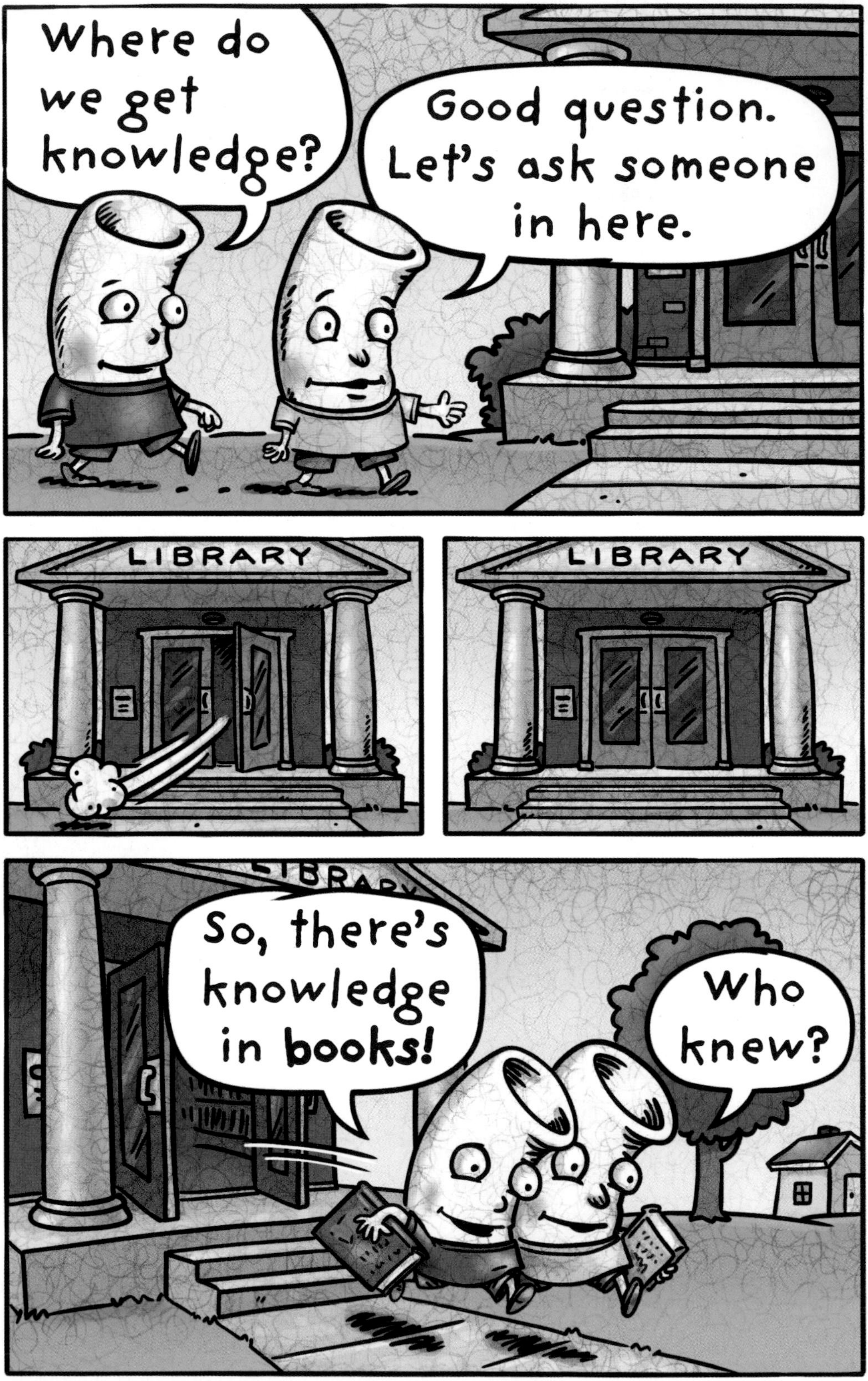
Where do we get knowledge?
Good question. Let's ask someone in here.
LIBRARY
LIBRARY
So, there's knowledge in **books**!
Who knew?

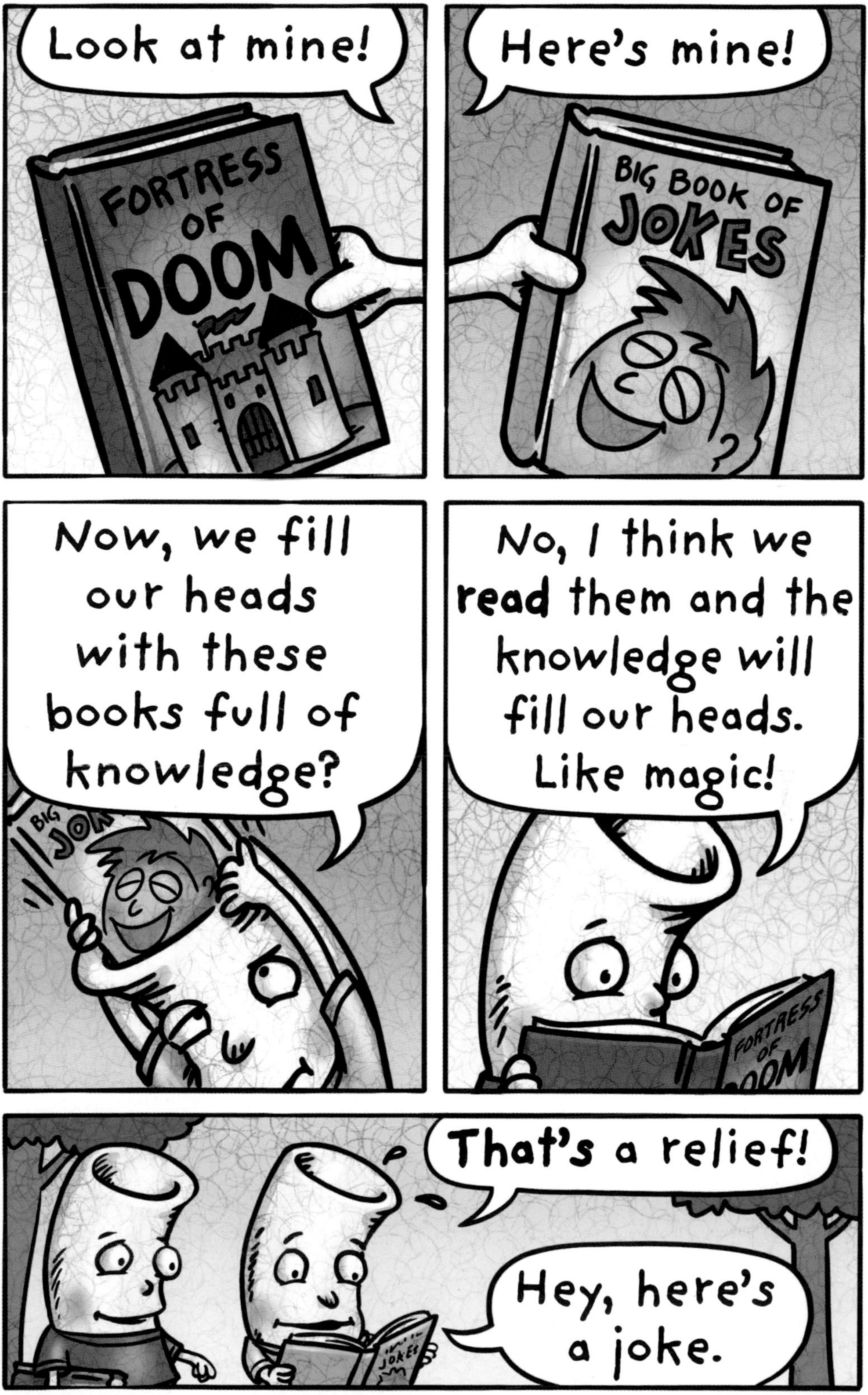
Look at mine!
FORTRESS OF DOOM
Here's mine!
BIG BOOK OF JOKES
Now, we fill our heads with these books full of knowledge?
No, I think we **read** them and the knowledge will fill our heads. Like magic!
FORTRESS OF
That's a relief!
Hey, here's a joke.
JOKES

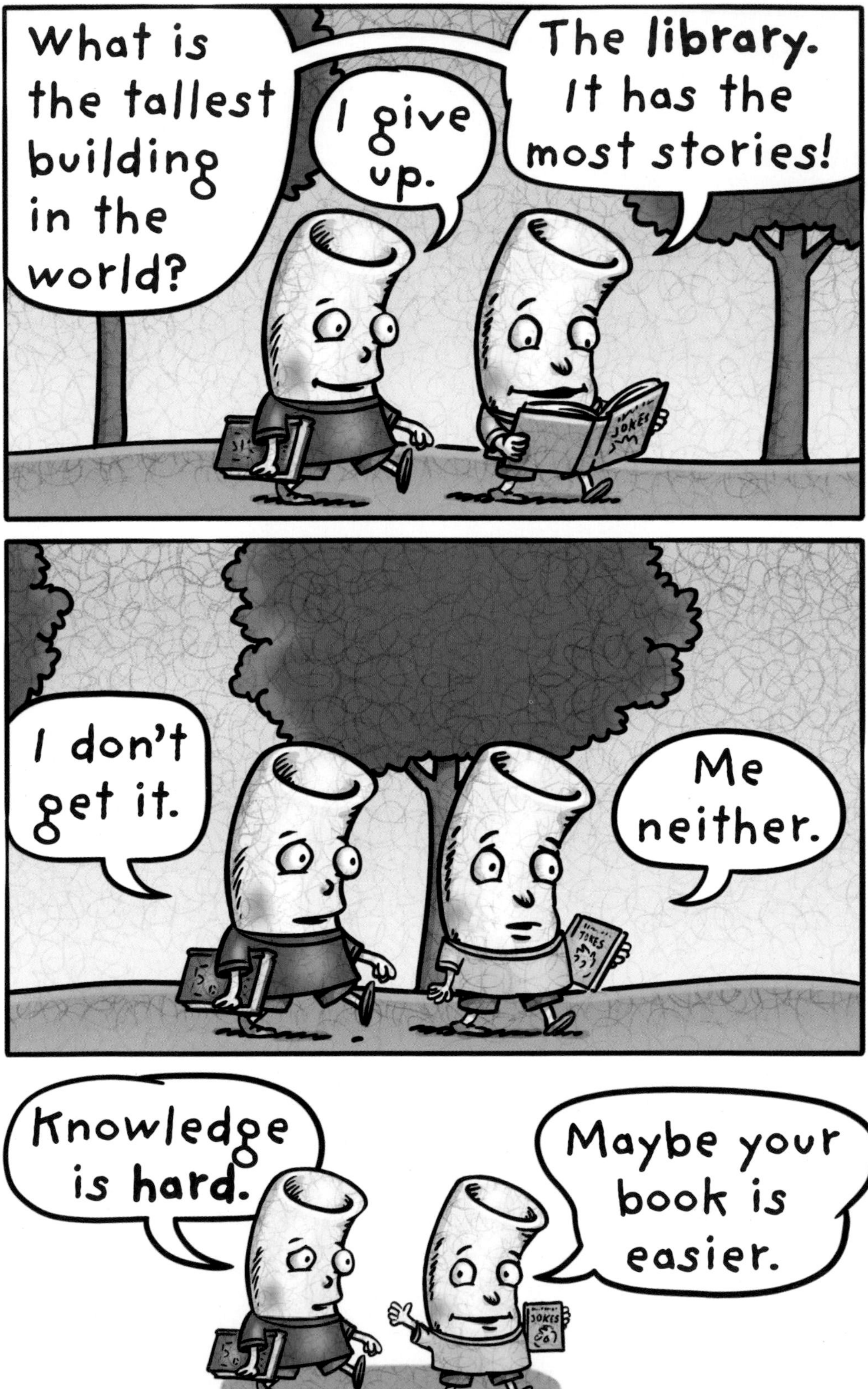
What is the tallest building in the world?
I give up.
The library. It has the most stories!
JOKES
I don't get it.
Me neither.
JOKES
Knowledge is hard.
Maybe your book is easier.
JOKES

NOODLEHEADS FORTRESS OF DOOM

CHAPTER 1

IF WE BUILD IT...

My book is all about the Fortress of **Doom!**

Hey, Mac, what's all this wood in our backyard?

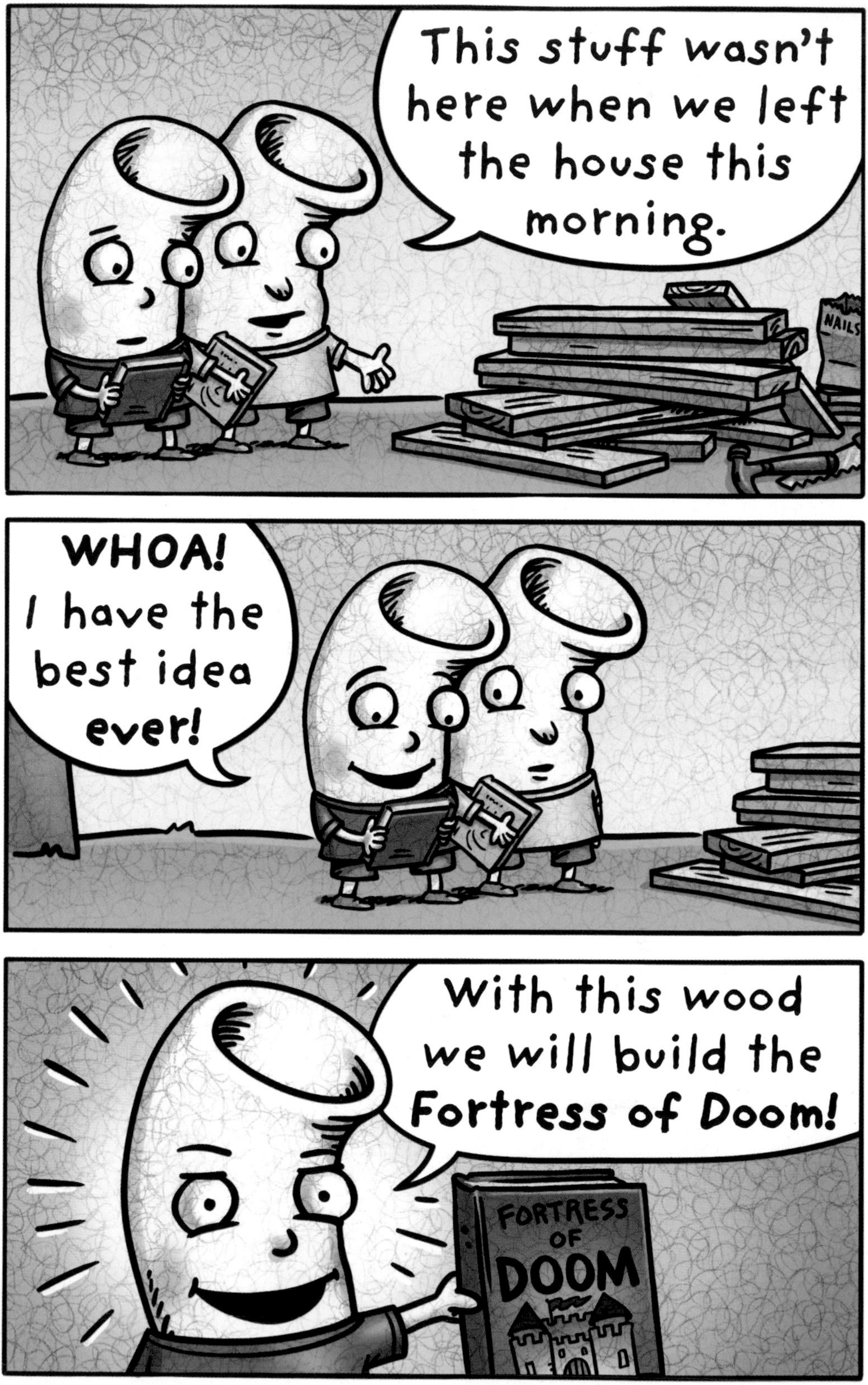
This stuff wasn't here when we left the house this morning.
NAILS
WHOA! I have the best idea ever!
With this wood we will build the Fortress of Doom!
FORTRESS OF DOOM

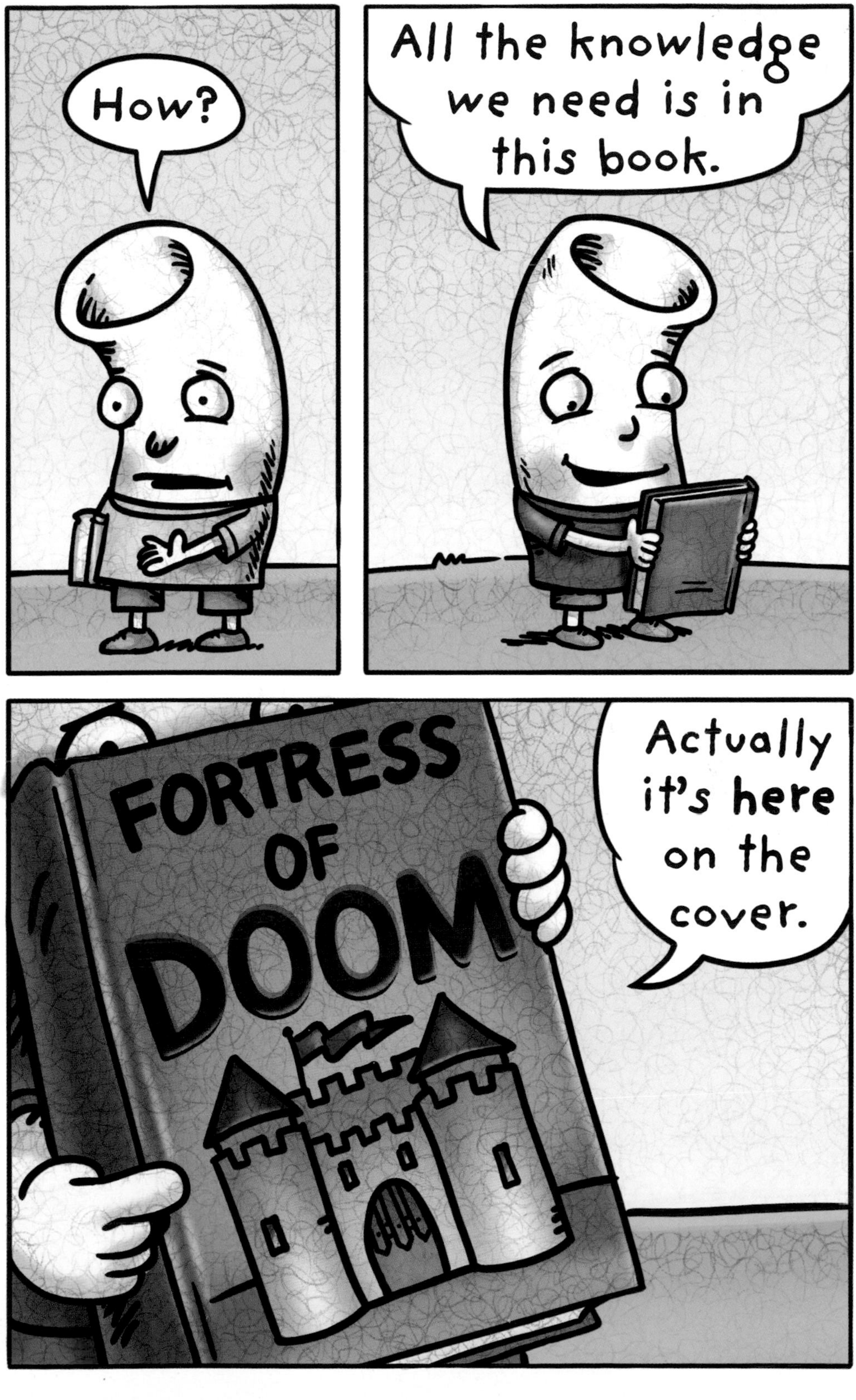
How?
All the knowledge we need is in this book.
FORTRESS OF DOOM
Actually it's here on the cover.

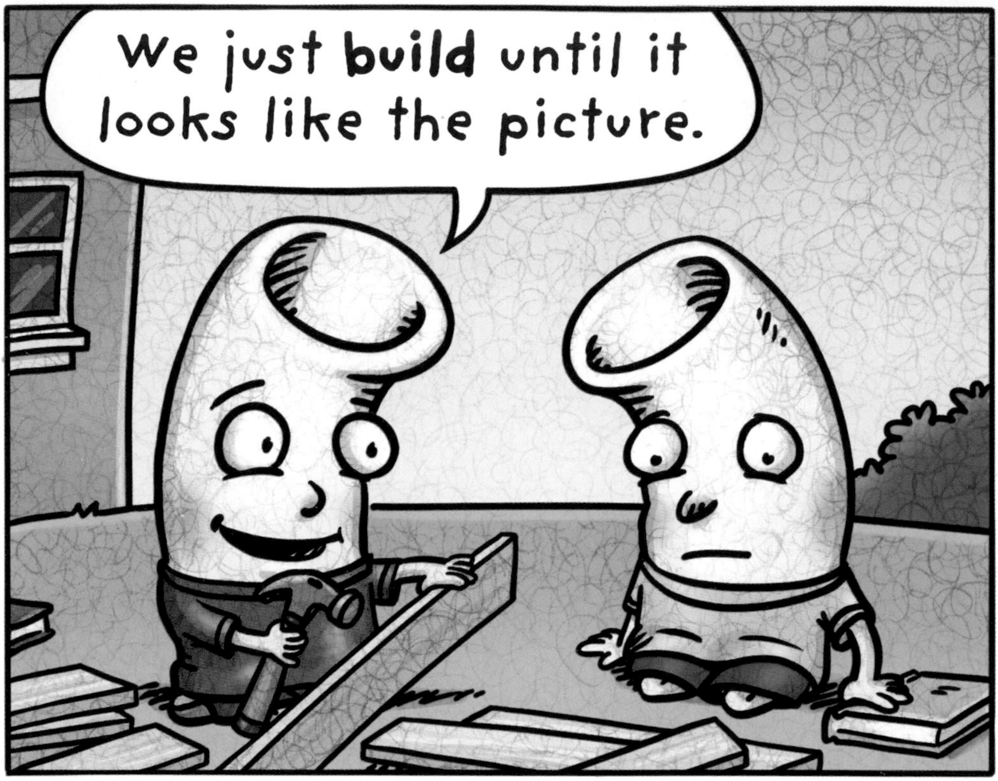
We just **build** until it looks like the picture.

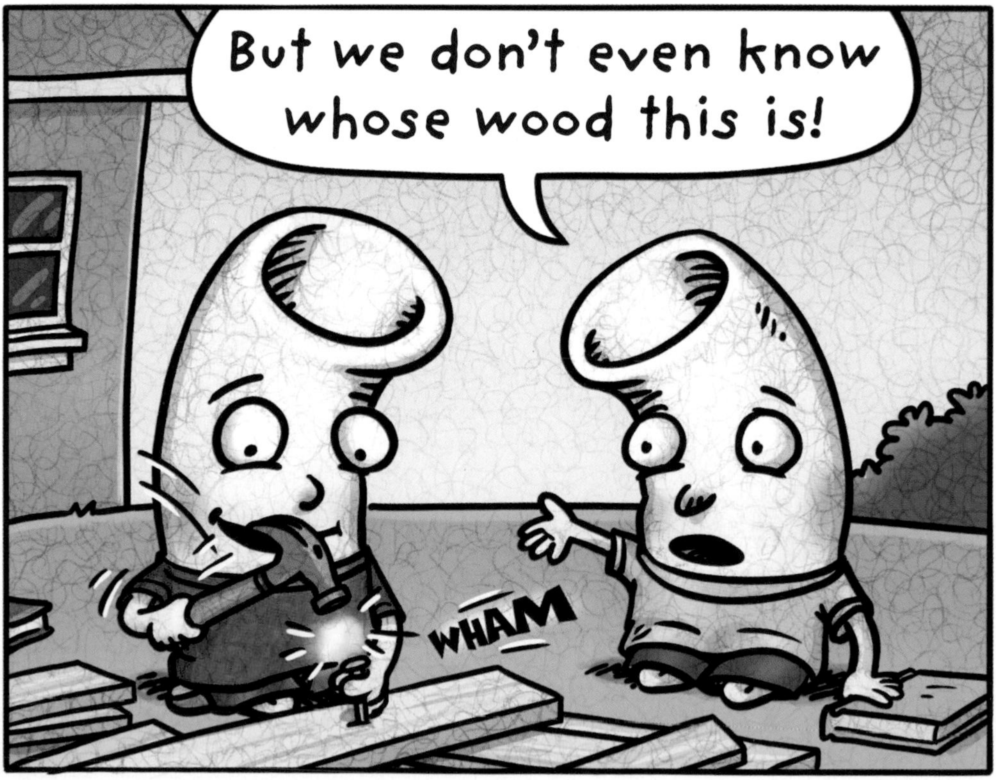
But we don't even know whose wood this is!
WHAM

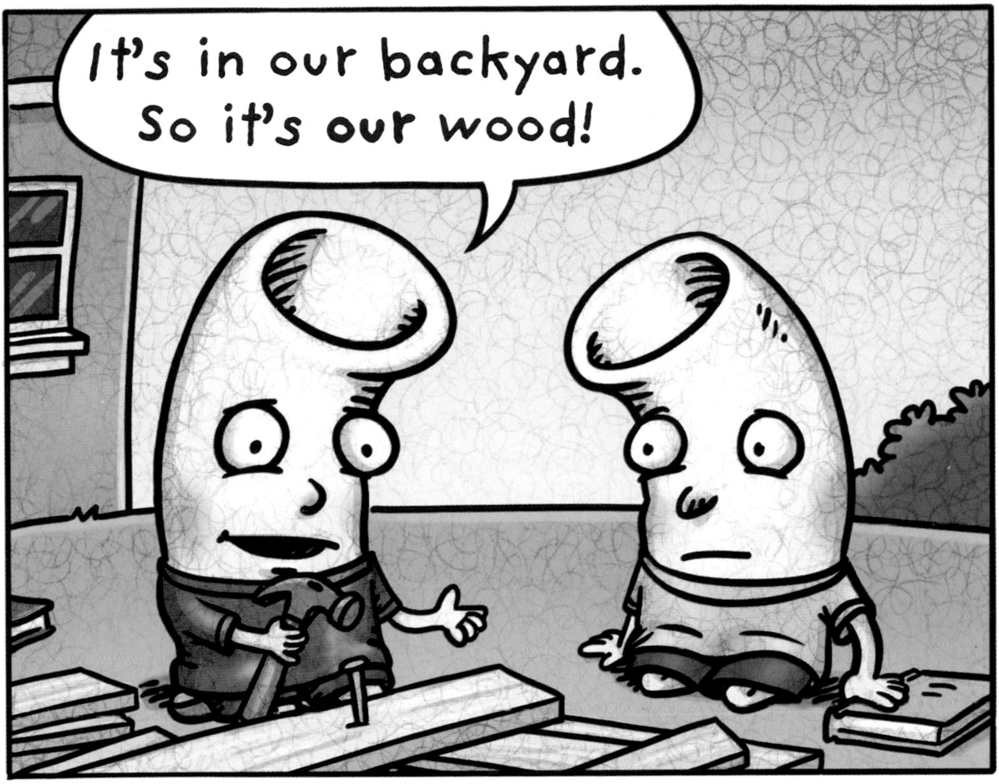
It's in our backyard.
So it's our wood!

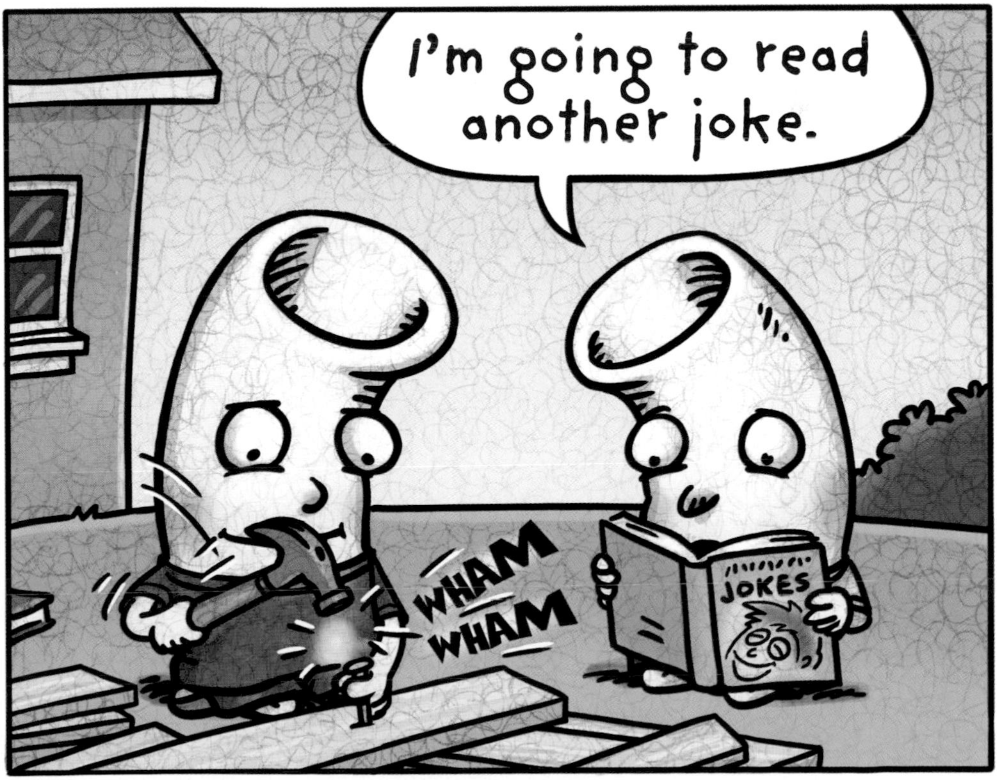
I'm going to read
another joke.
WHAM
WHAM
JOKES

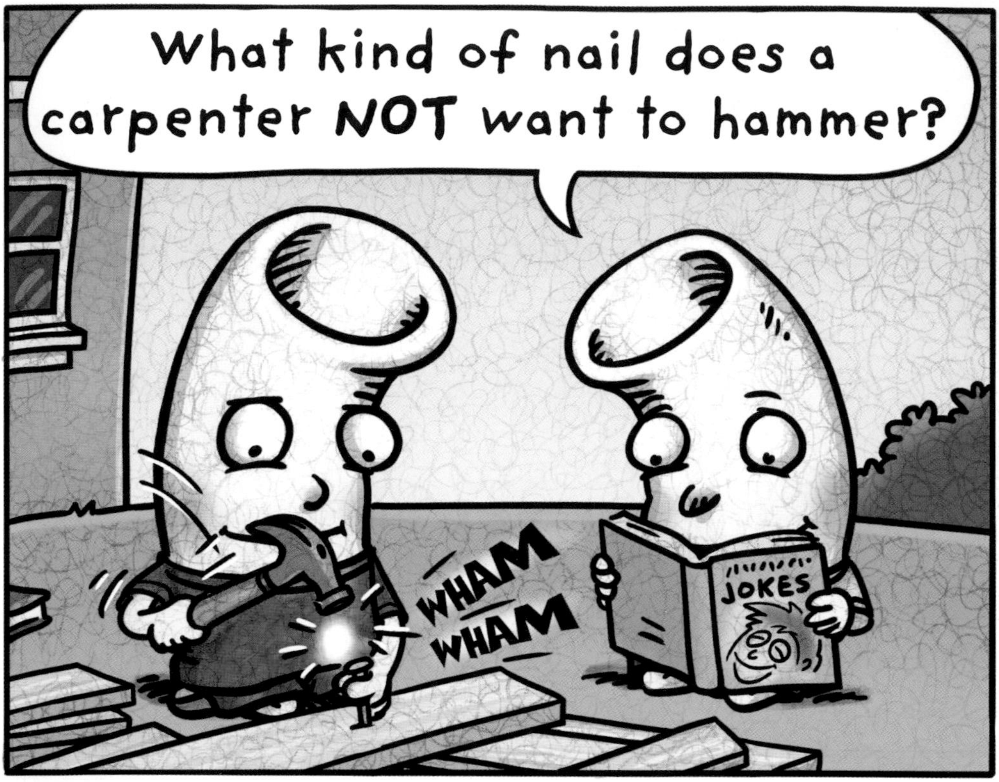
What kind of nail does a carpenter NOT want to hammer?
WHAM
WHAM
JOKES

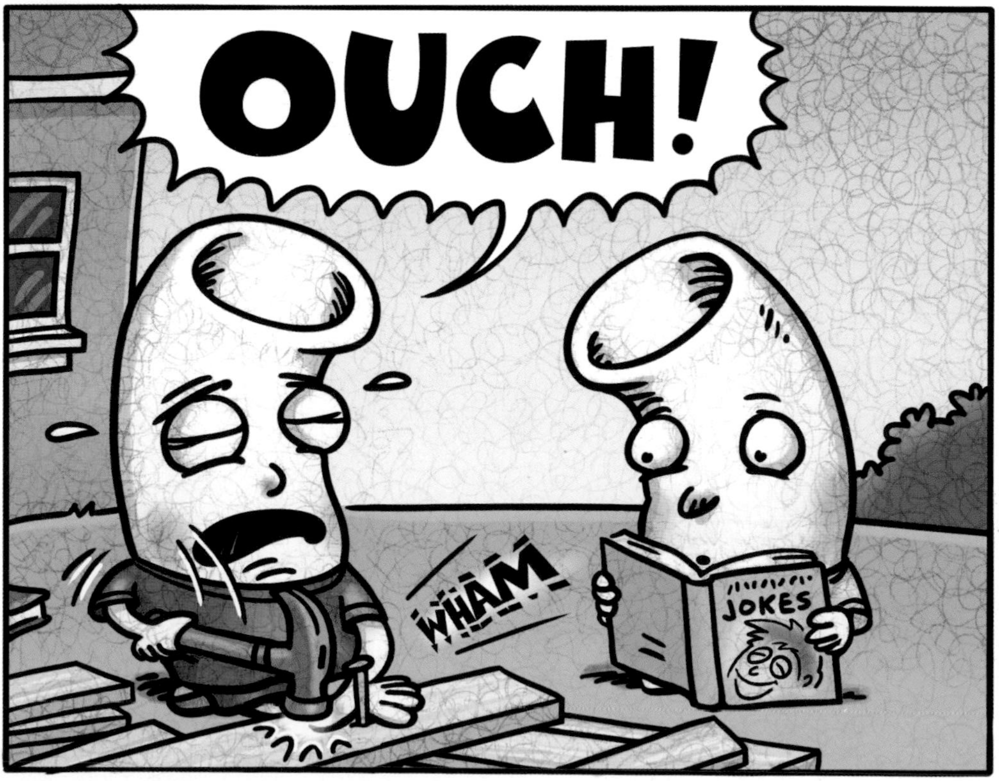
OUCH!
WHAM
JOKES

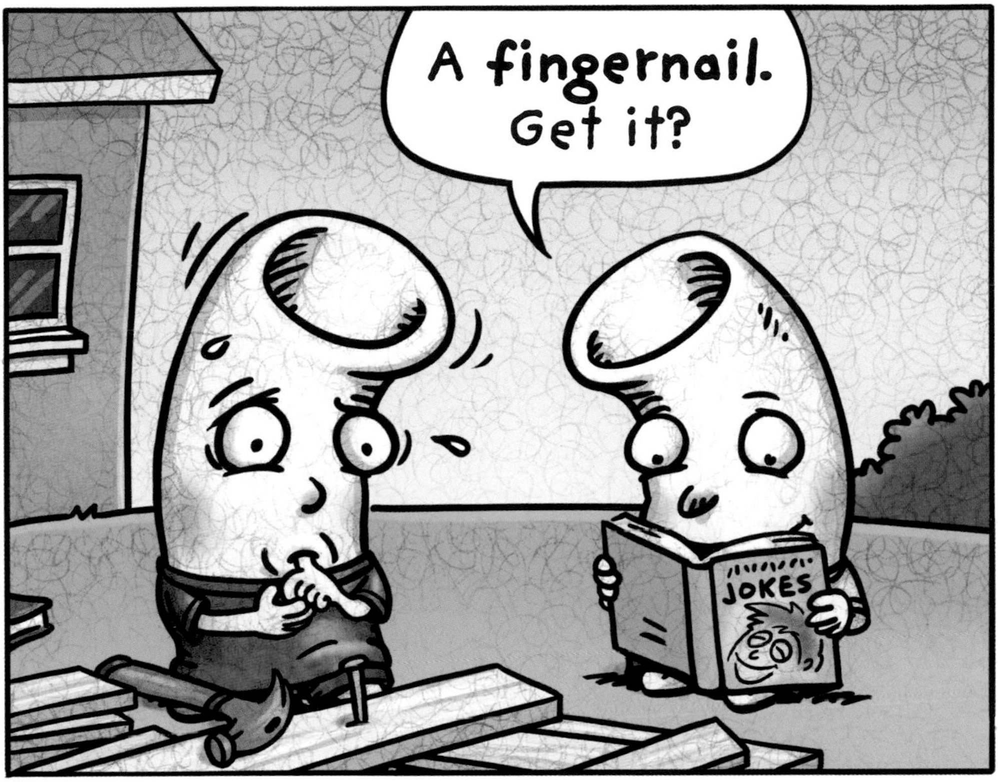
A fingernail. Get it?
JOKES

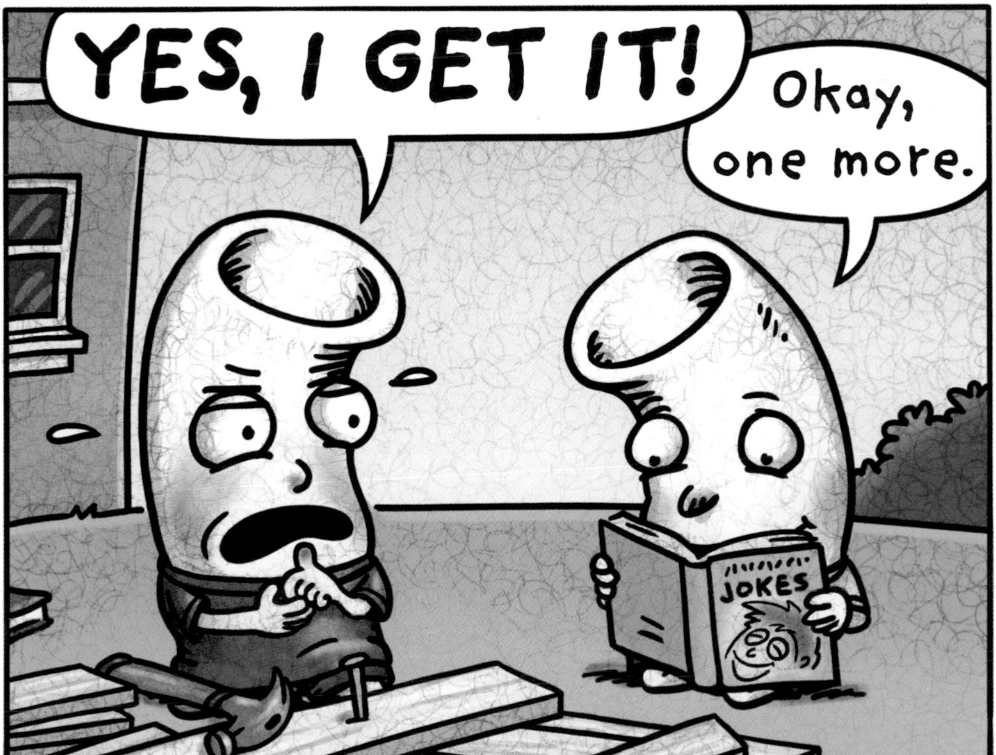
YES, I GET IT!
Okay, one more.
JOKES

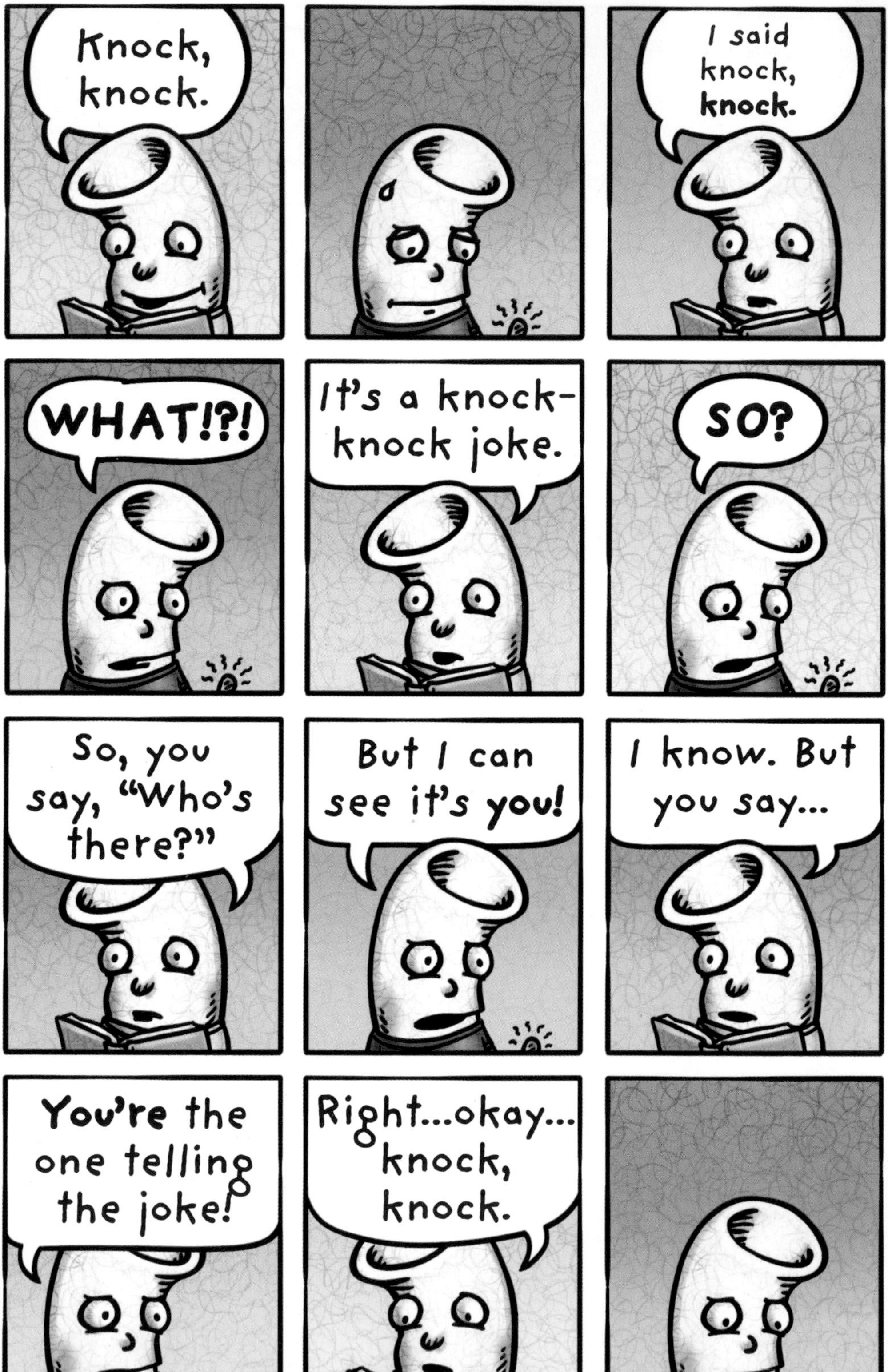
Knock, knock.
I said knock, **knock.**
WHAT!?!
It's a knock-knock joke.
SO?
So, you say, "Who's there?"
But I can see it's *you!*
I know. But you say...
You're the one telling the joke!
Right...okay... knock, knock.

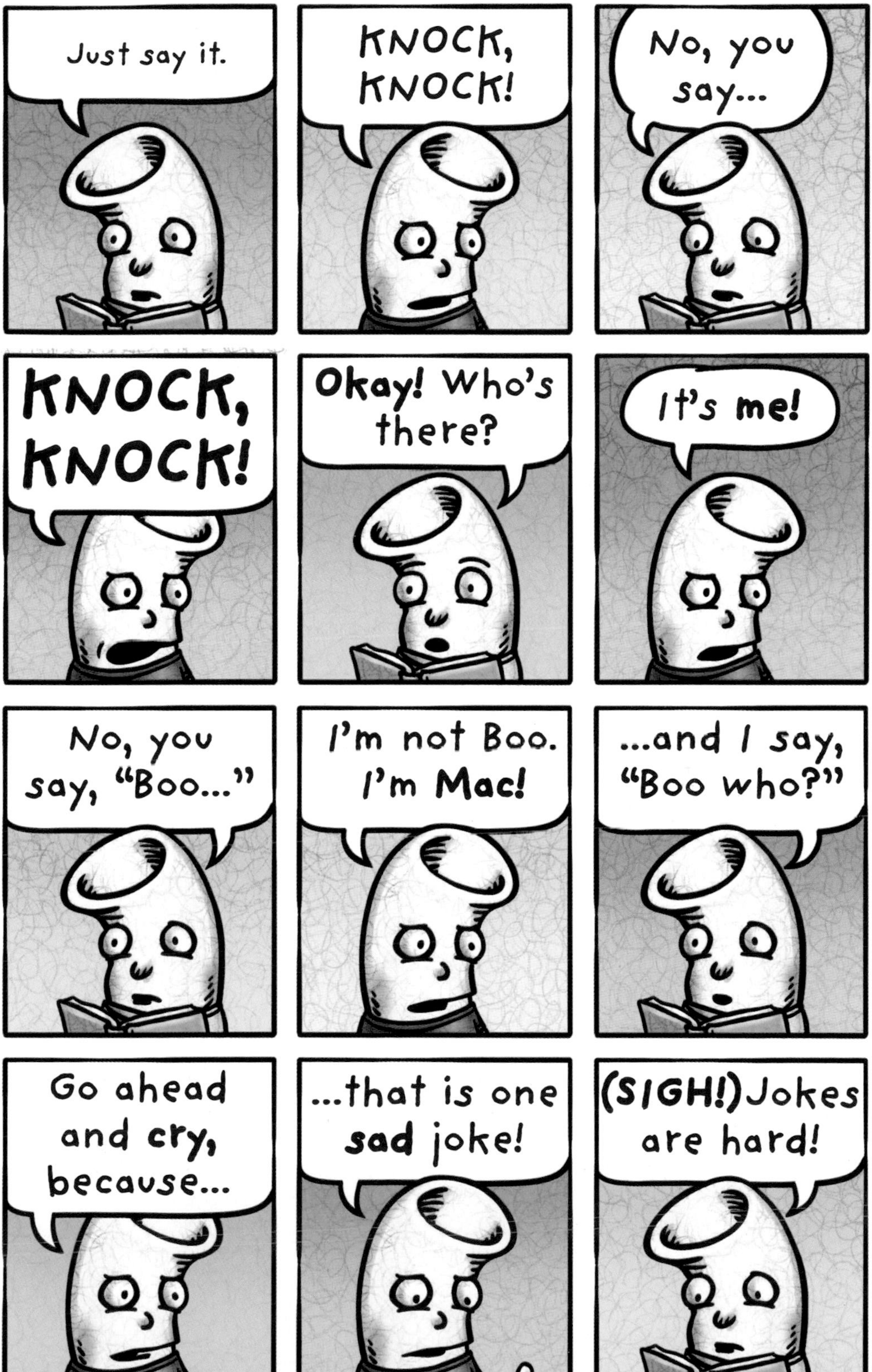
Just say it.
KNOCK, KNOCK!
No, you say...
KNOCK, KNOCK!
Okay! Who's there?
It's me!
No, you say, "Boo..."
I'm not Boo. I'm Mac!
...and I say, "Boo who?"
Go ahead and cry, because...
...that is one sad joke!
(SIGH!) Jokes are hard!

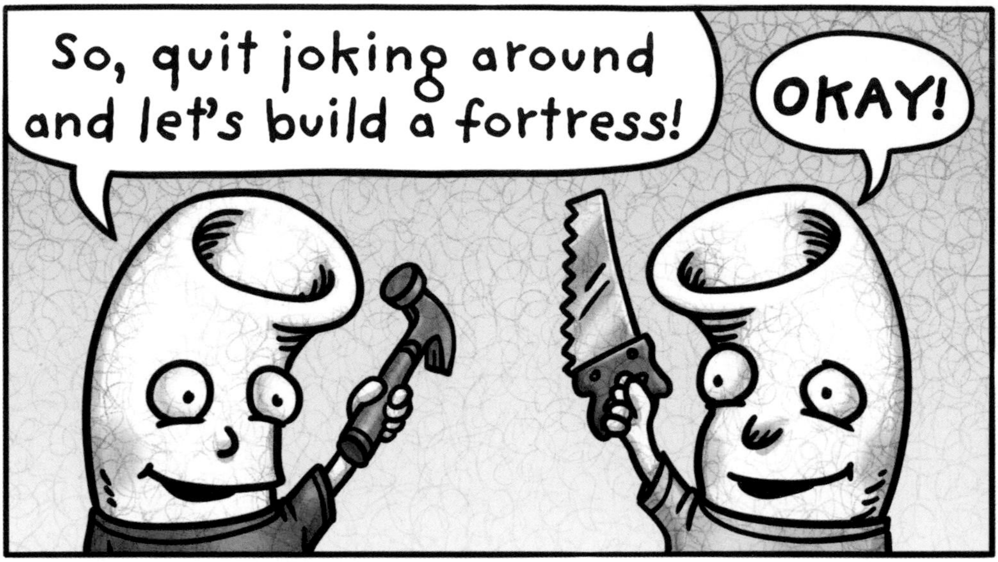
So, quit joking around and let's build a fortress!
OKAY!

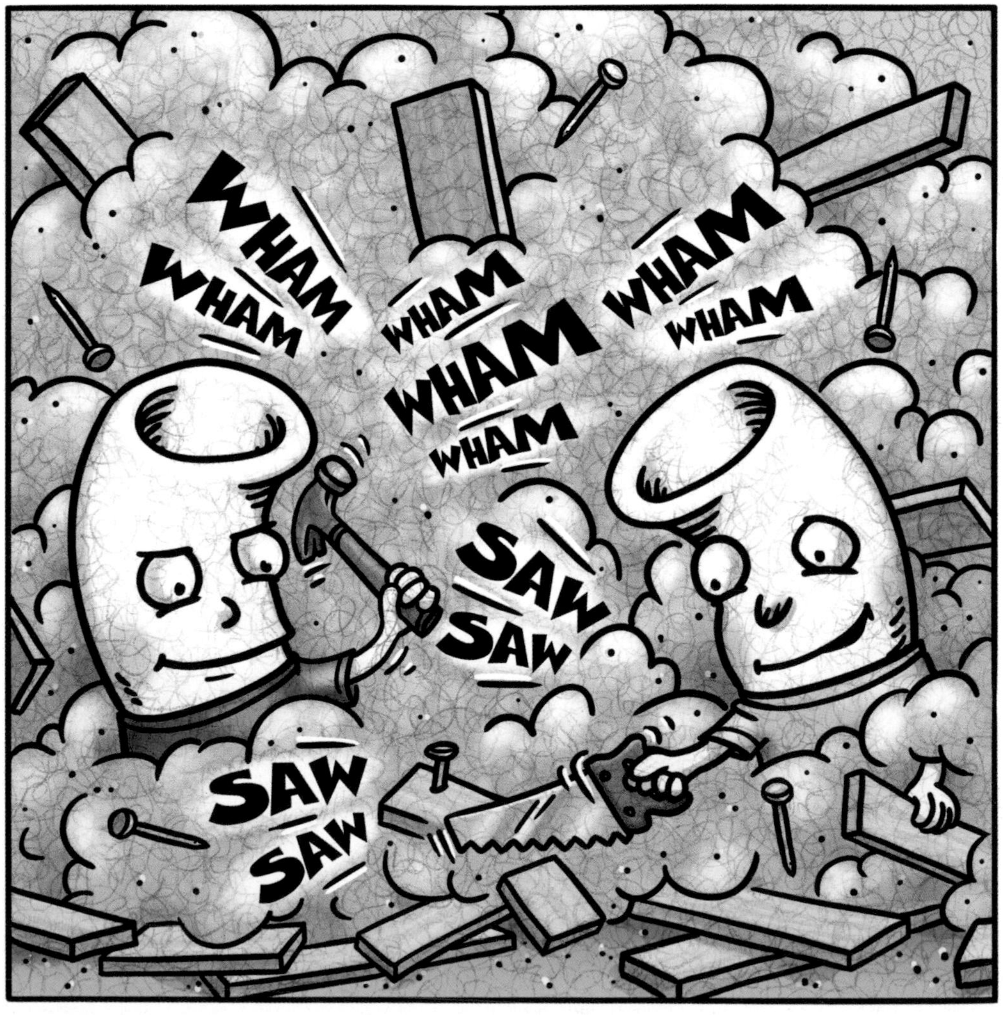
WHAM
WHAM
WHAM
WHAM
WHAM
WHAM
WHAM
WHAM
SAW
SAW
SAW
SAW

NOODLEHEADS
FORTRESS OF DOOM

GUARDING THE DOOR

Hours later...

YAY! WE FINISHED!

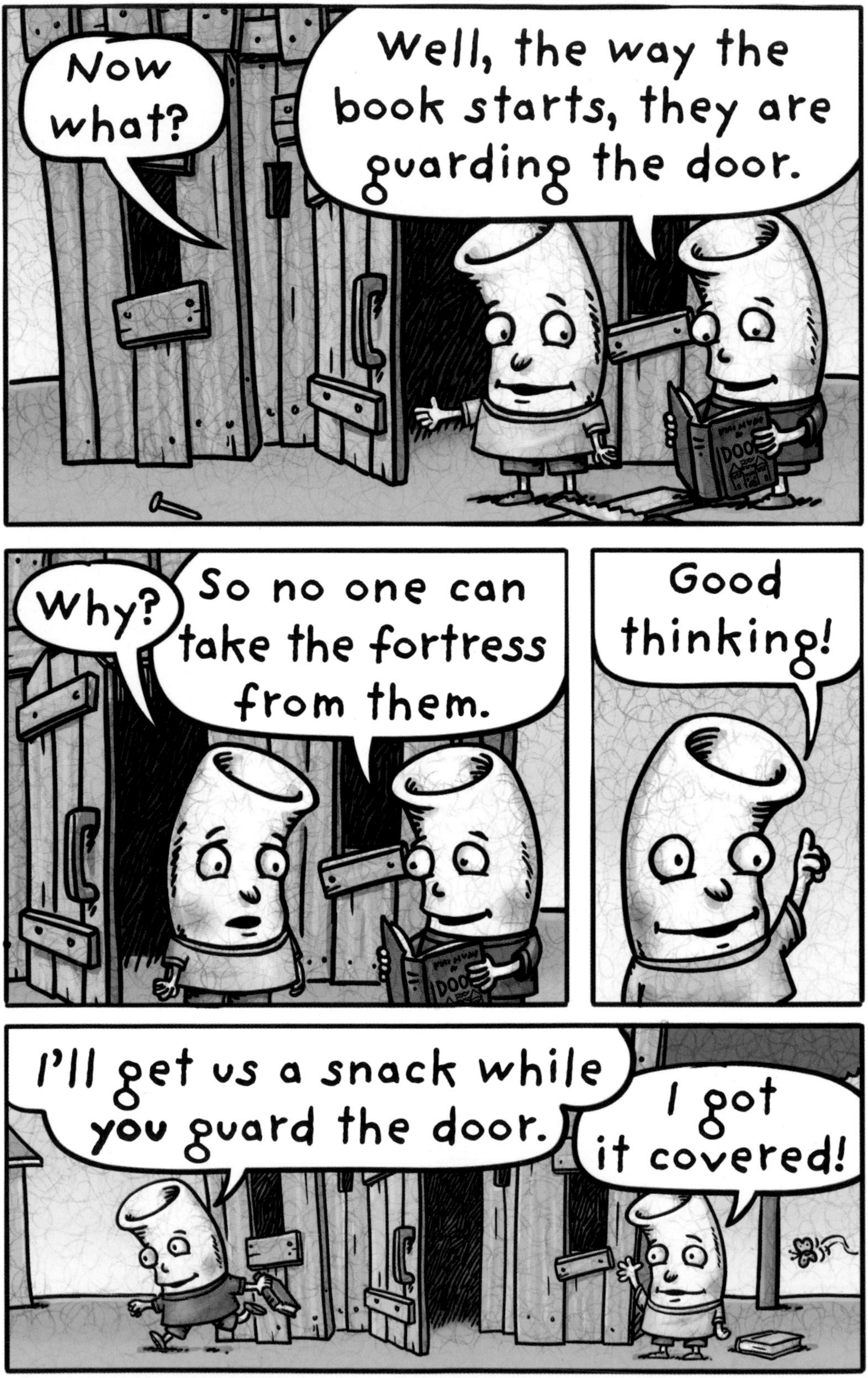
Now what?
Well, the way the book starts, they are guarding the door.
Why?
So no one can take the fortress from them.
Good thinking!
I'll get us a snack while you guard the door.
I got it covered!

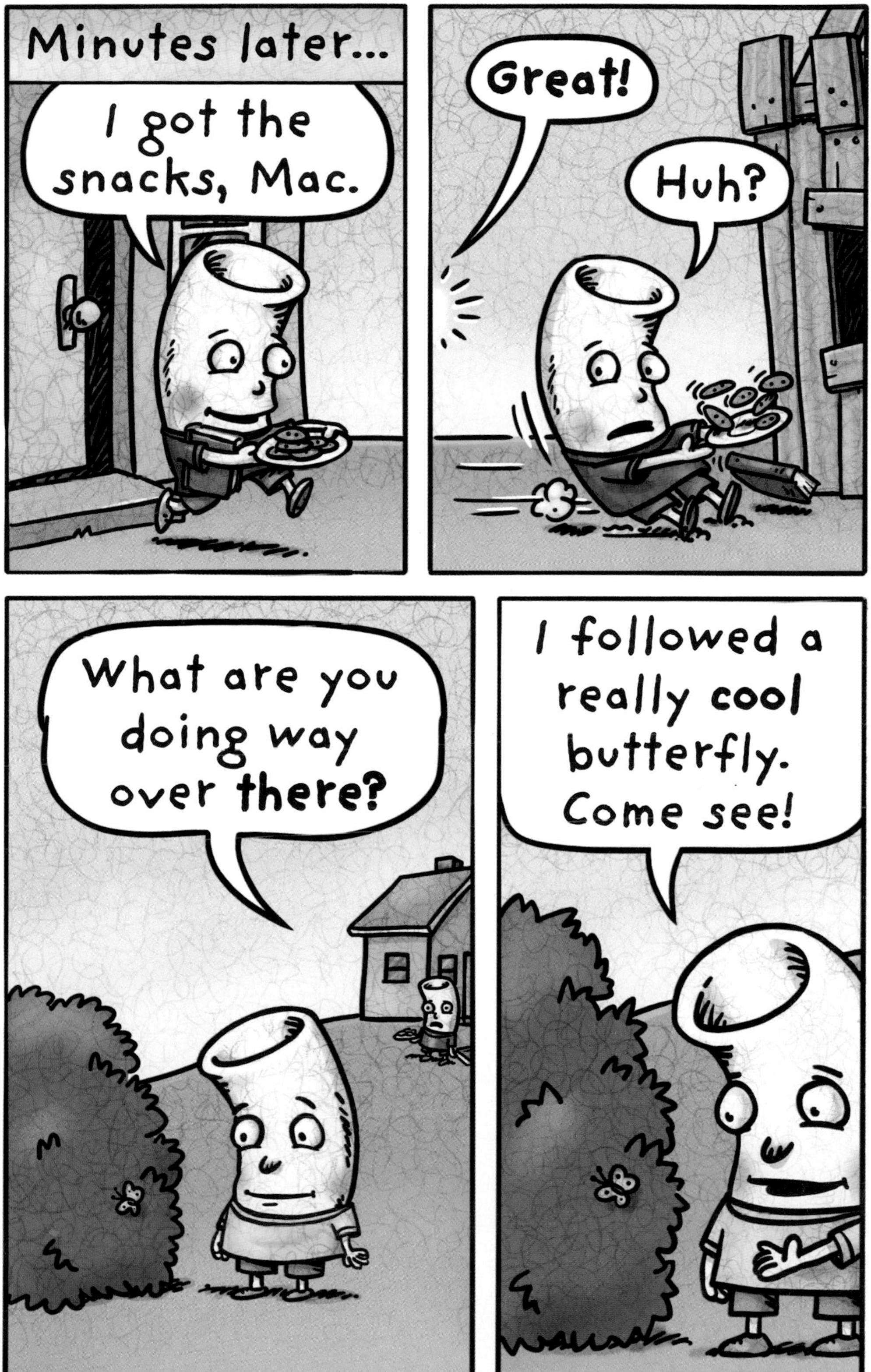
Minutes later...
I got the snacks, Mac.
Great!
Huh?
What are you doing way over there?
I followed a really cool butterfly. Come see!

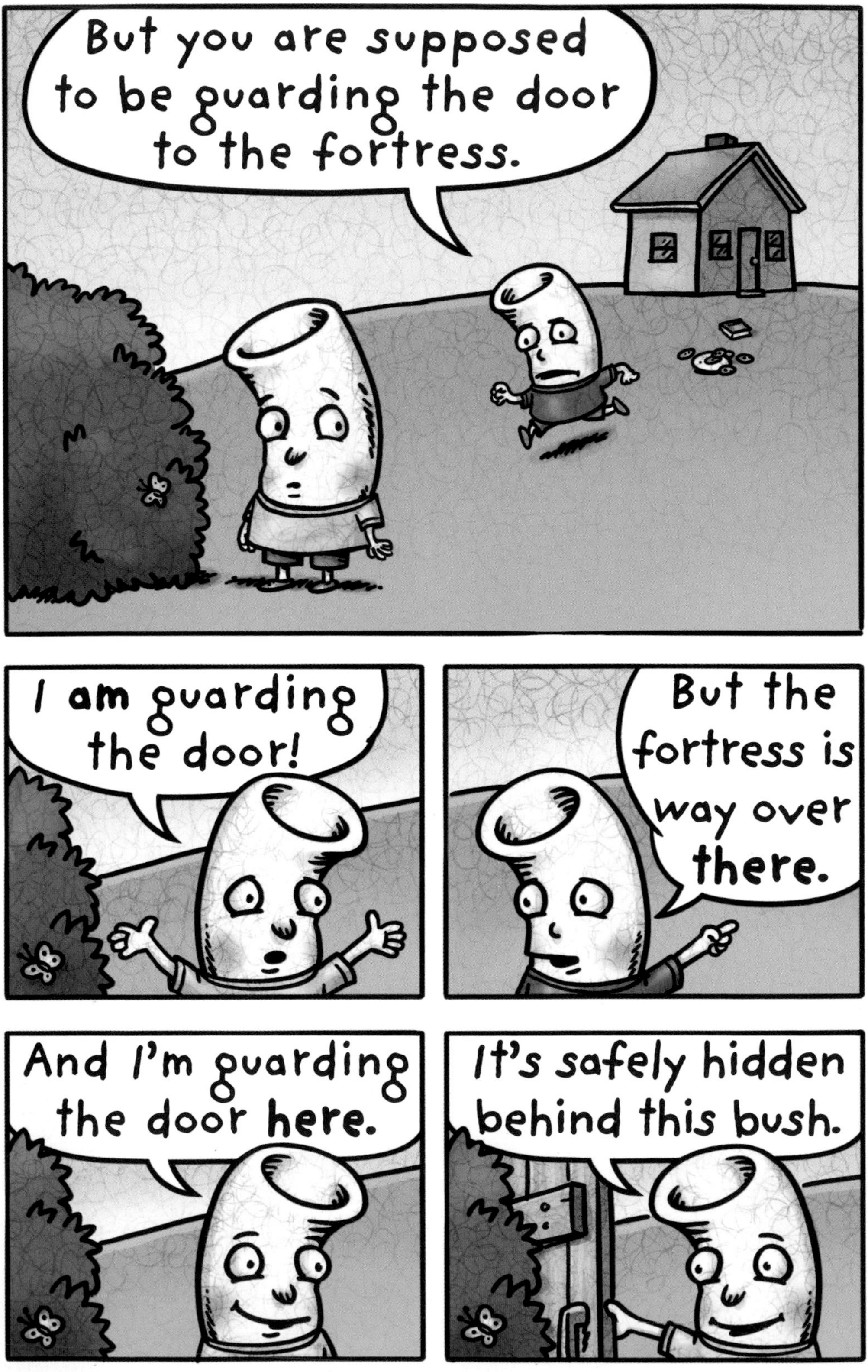
But you are supposed to be guarding the door to the fortress.
I am guarding the door!
But the fortress is way over there.
And I'm guarding the door here.
It's safely hidden behind this bush.

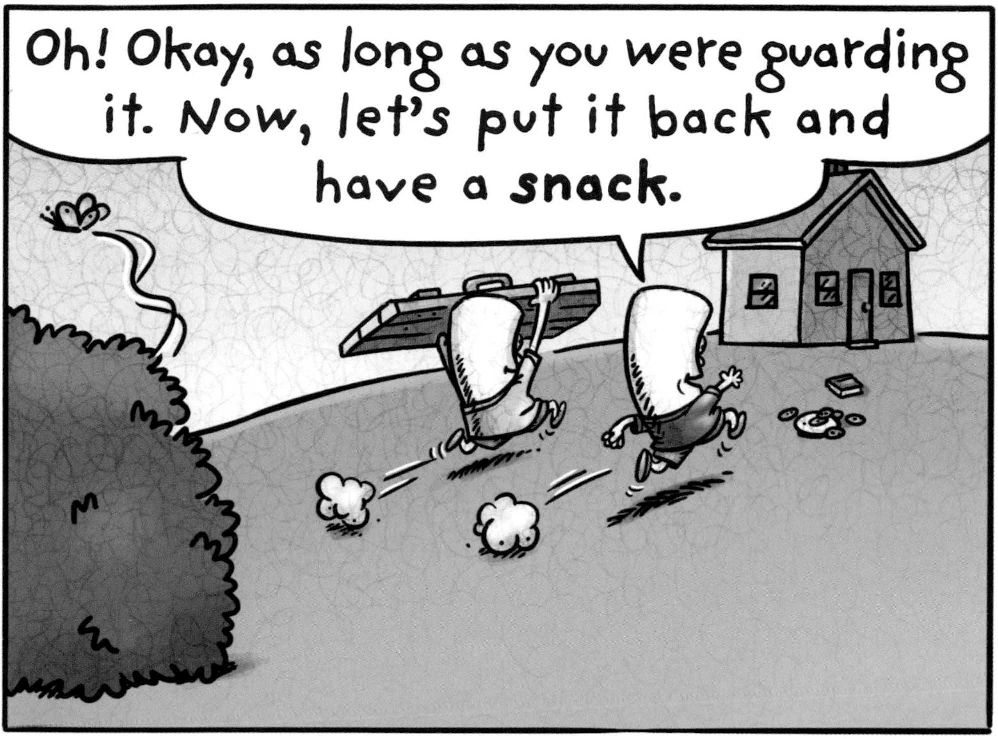
Oh! Okay, as long as you were guarding it. Now, let's put it back and have a snack.

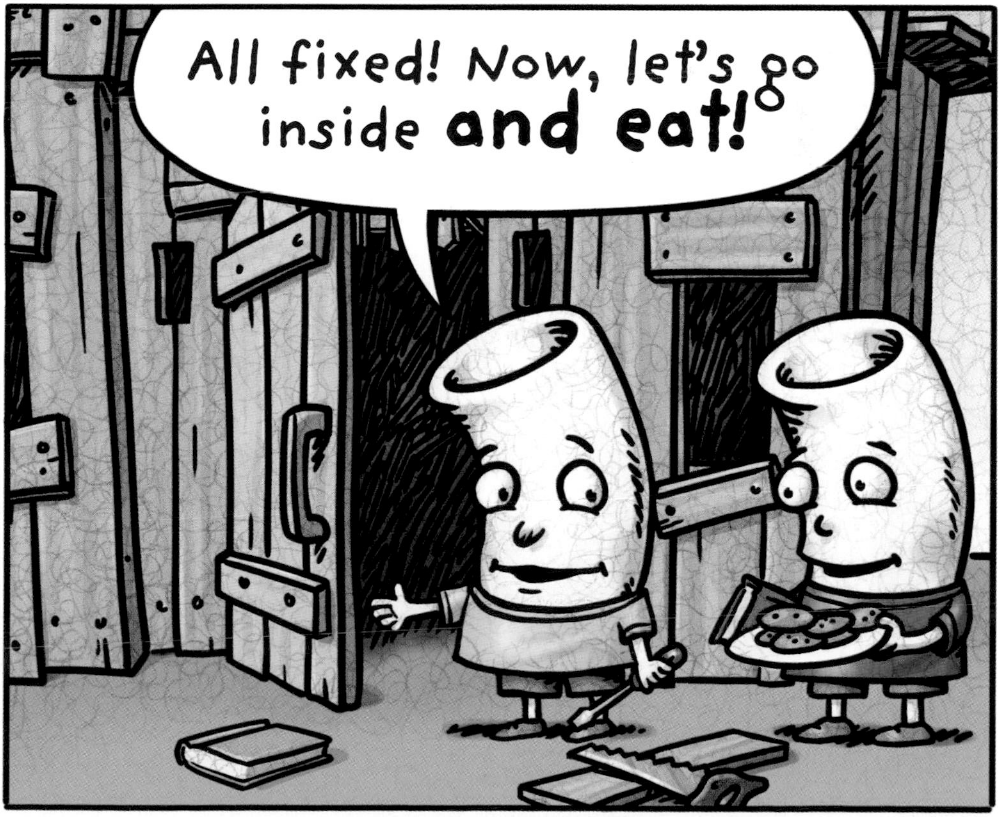
All fixed! Now, let's go inside and eat!

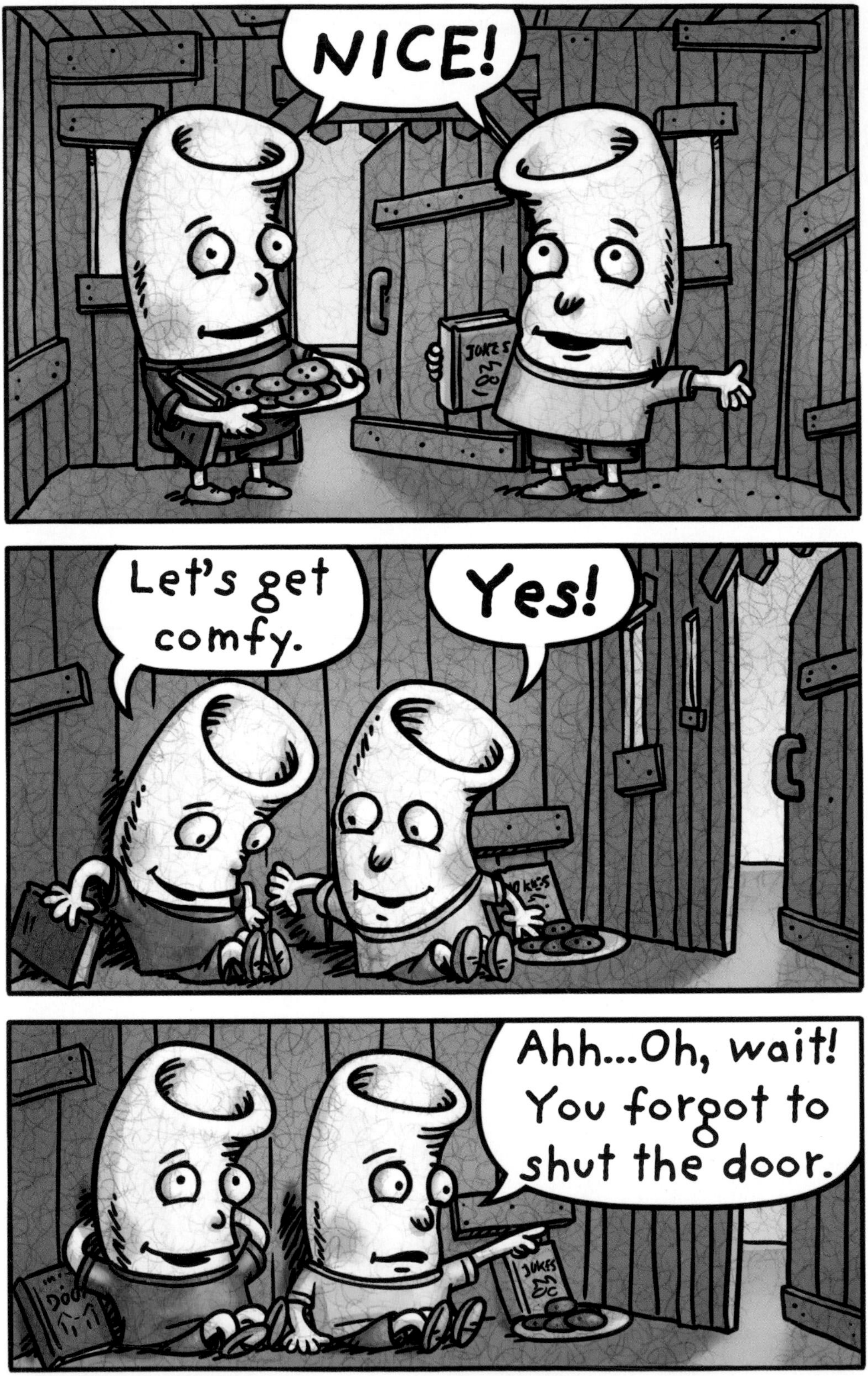
NICE!
Let's get comfy.
Yes!
Ahh...Oh, wait! You forgot to shut the door.

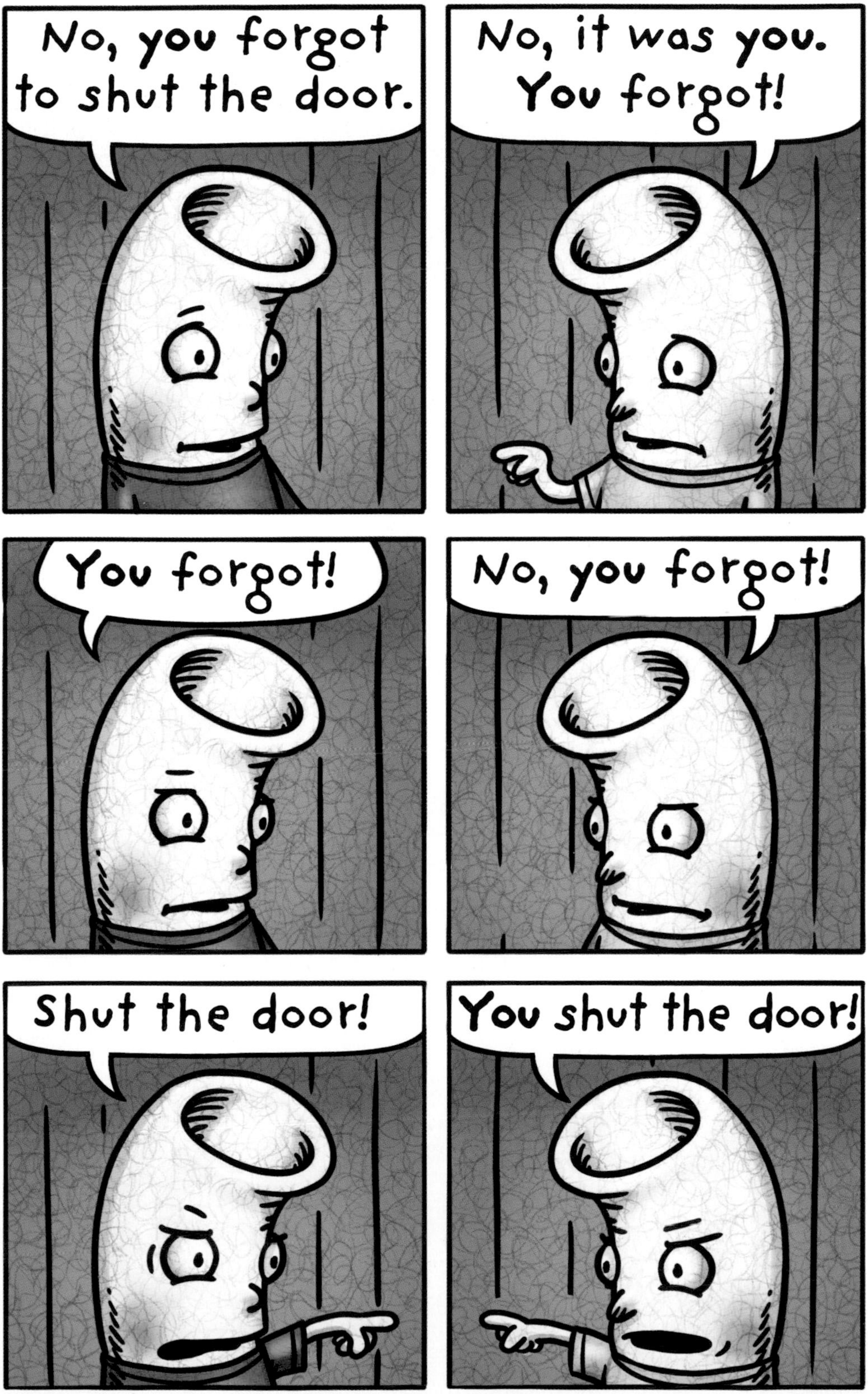
No, you forgot to shut the door.
No, it was you. You forgot!
You forgot!
No, you forgot!
Shut the door!
You shut the door!

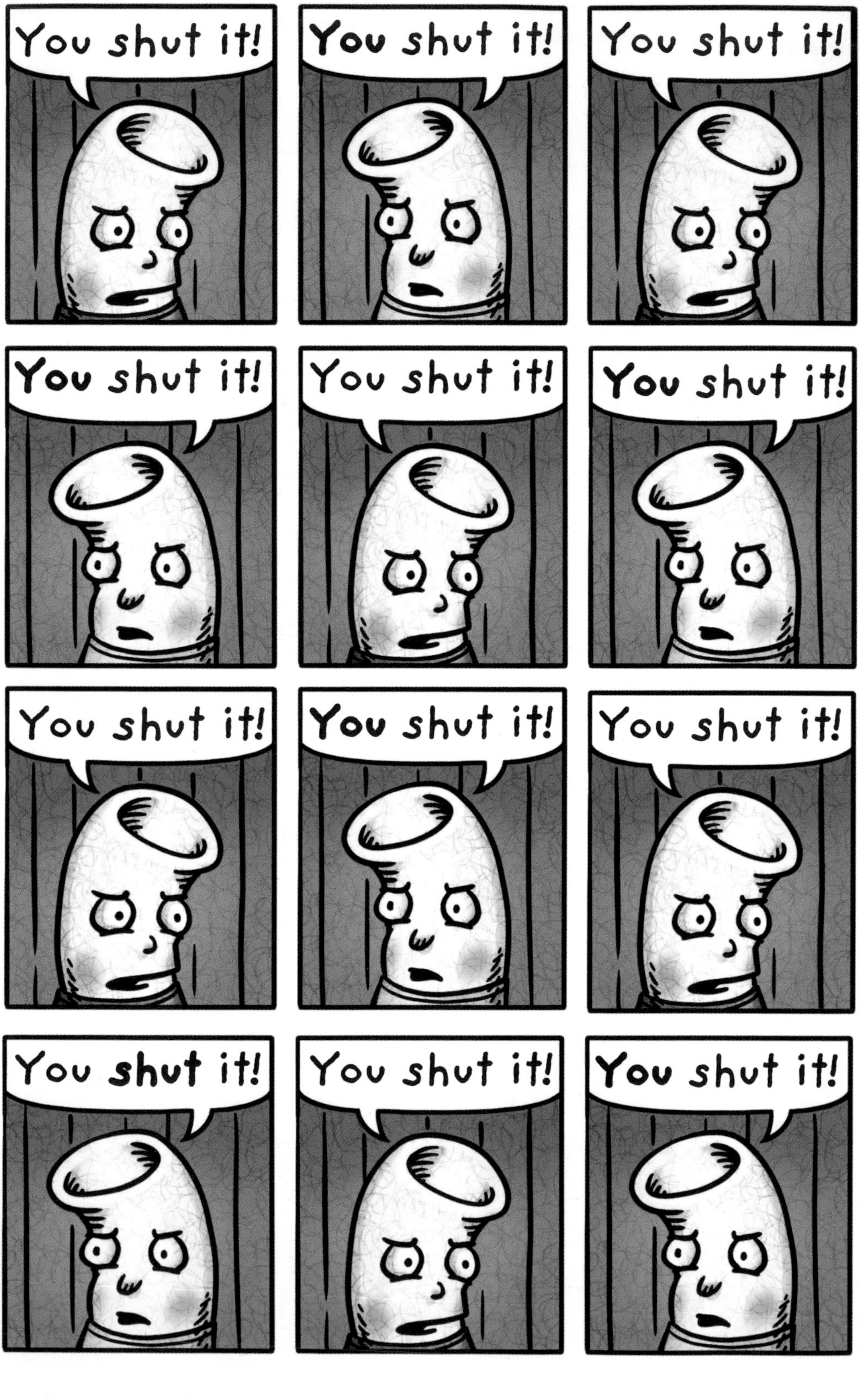
You shut it!
You shut it!
You shut it!
You shut it!
You shut it!
You shut it!
You shut it!
You shut it!
You shut it!
You shut it!
You shut it!
You shut it!

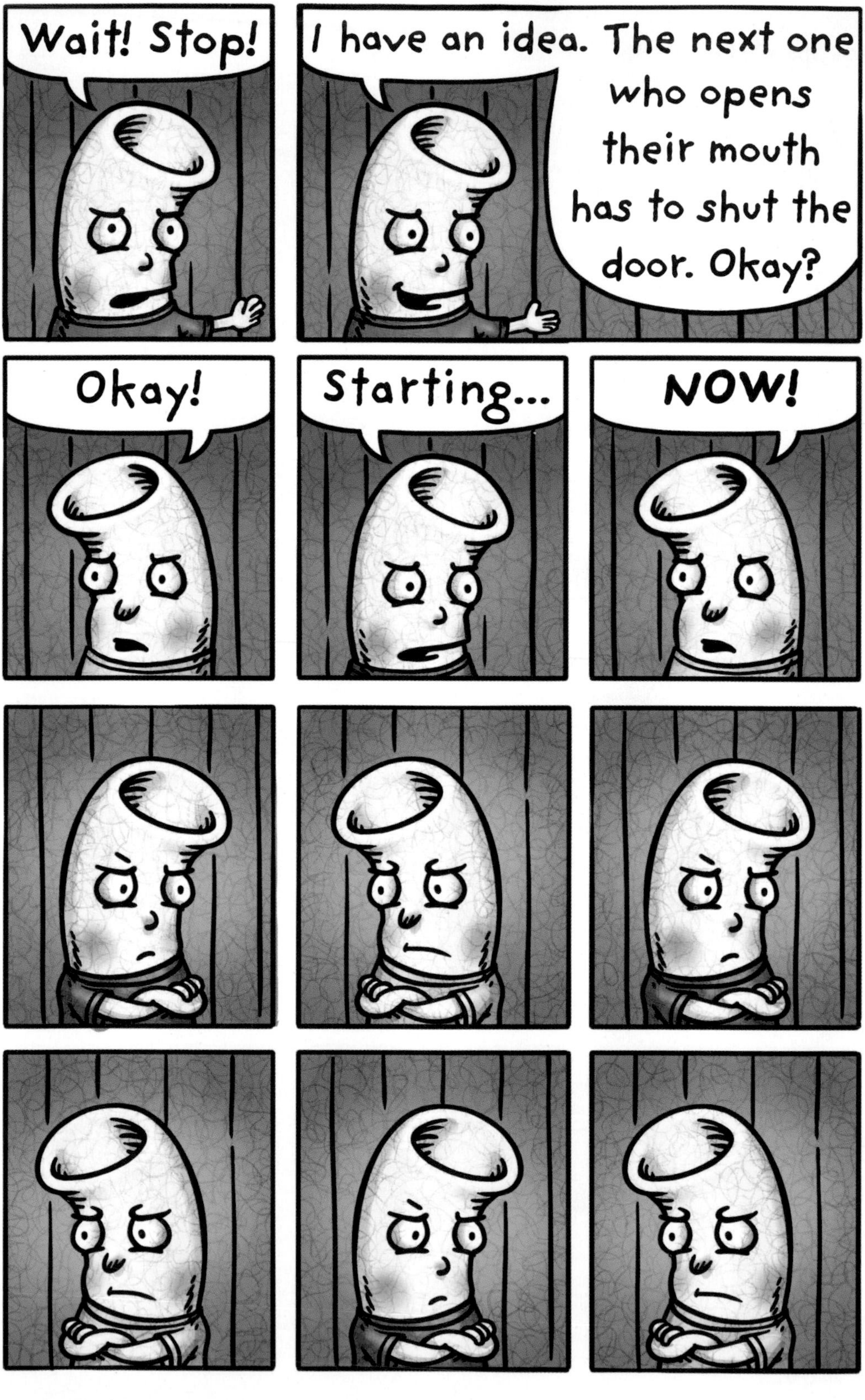
Wait! Stop!
I have an idea. The next one who opens their mouth has to shut the door. Okay?
Okay!
Starting...
NOW!

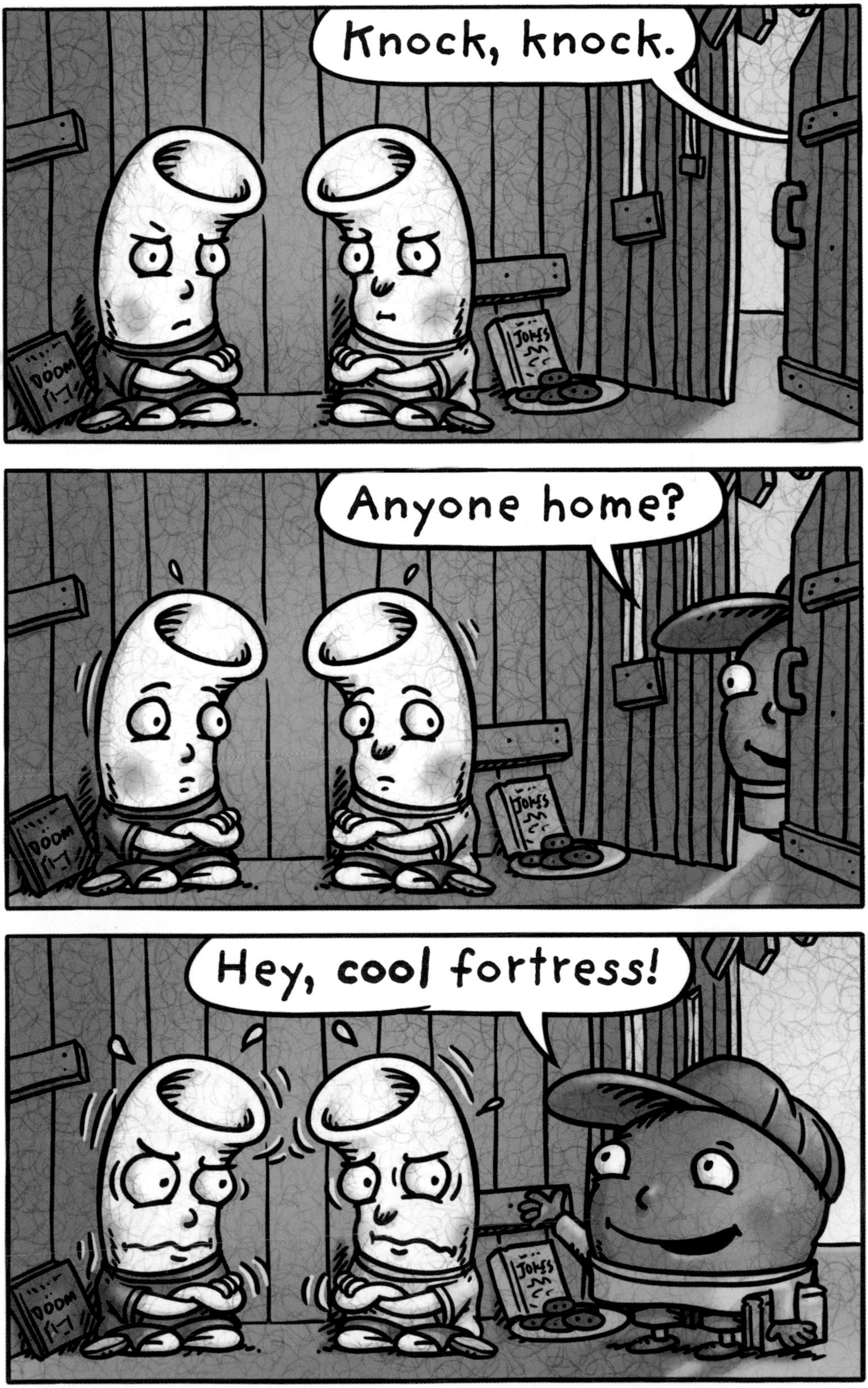
Knock, knock.
Anyone home?
Hey, cool fortress!

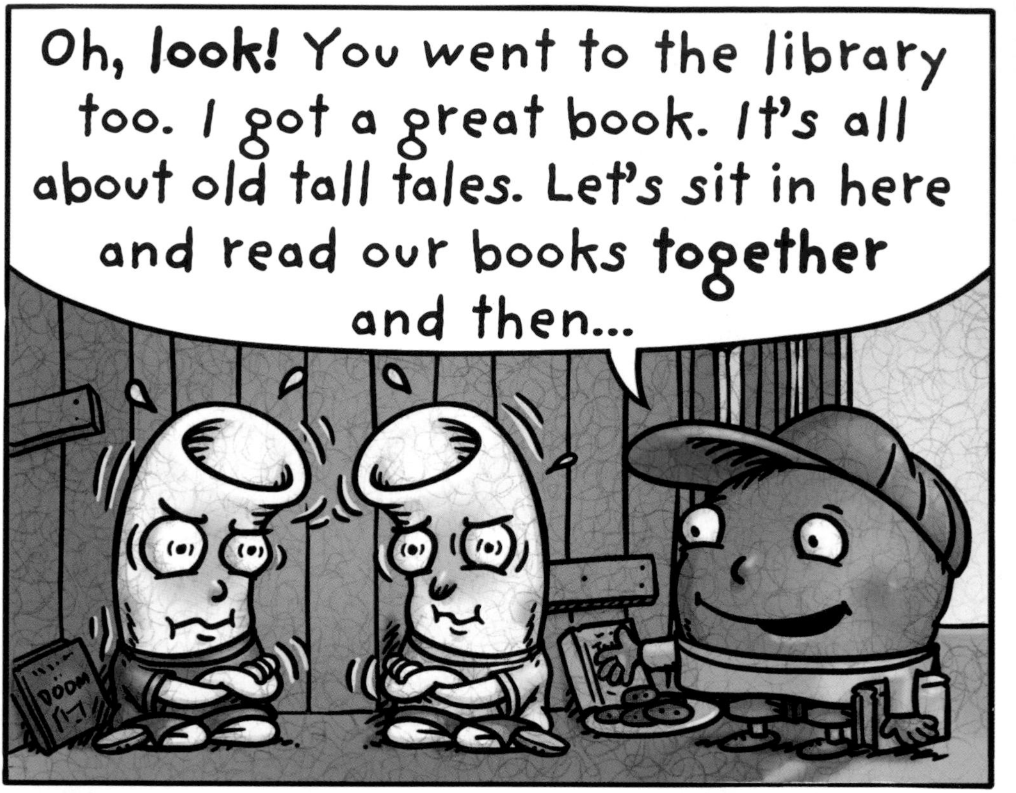
Oh, look! You went to the library too. I got a great book. It's all about old tall tales. Let's sit in here and read our books together and then...
DOOM

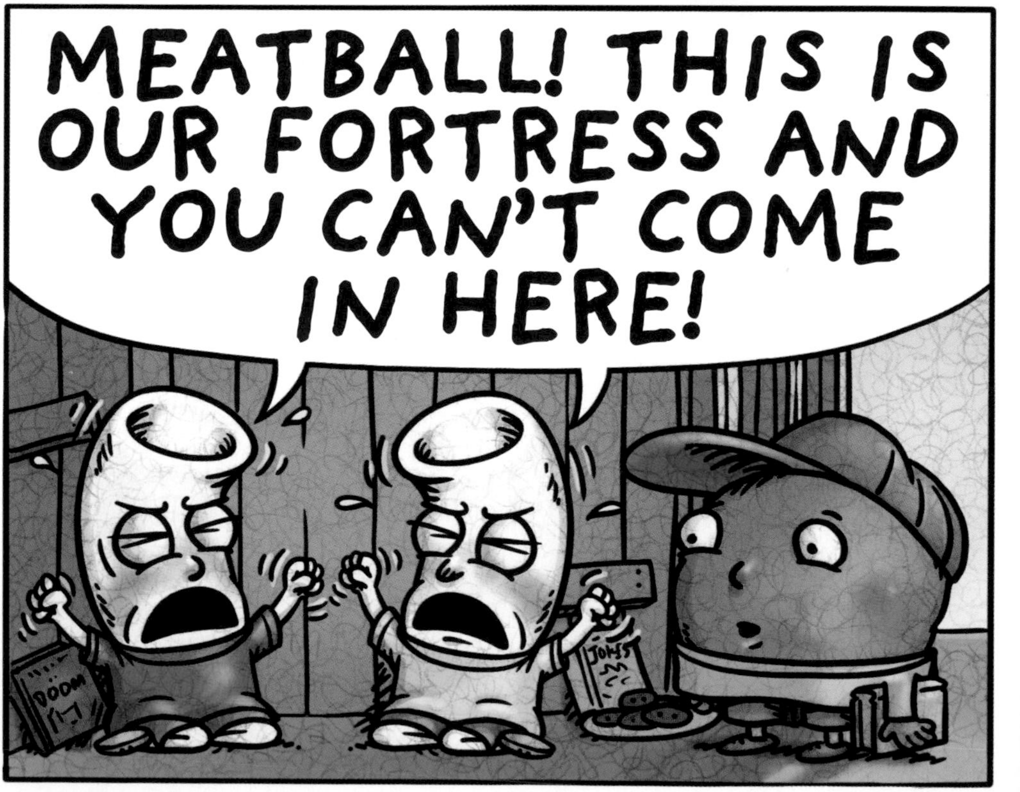
MEATBALL! THIS IS OUR FORTRESS AND YOU CAN'T COME IN HERE!
DOOM

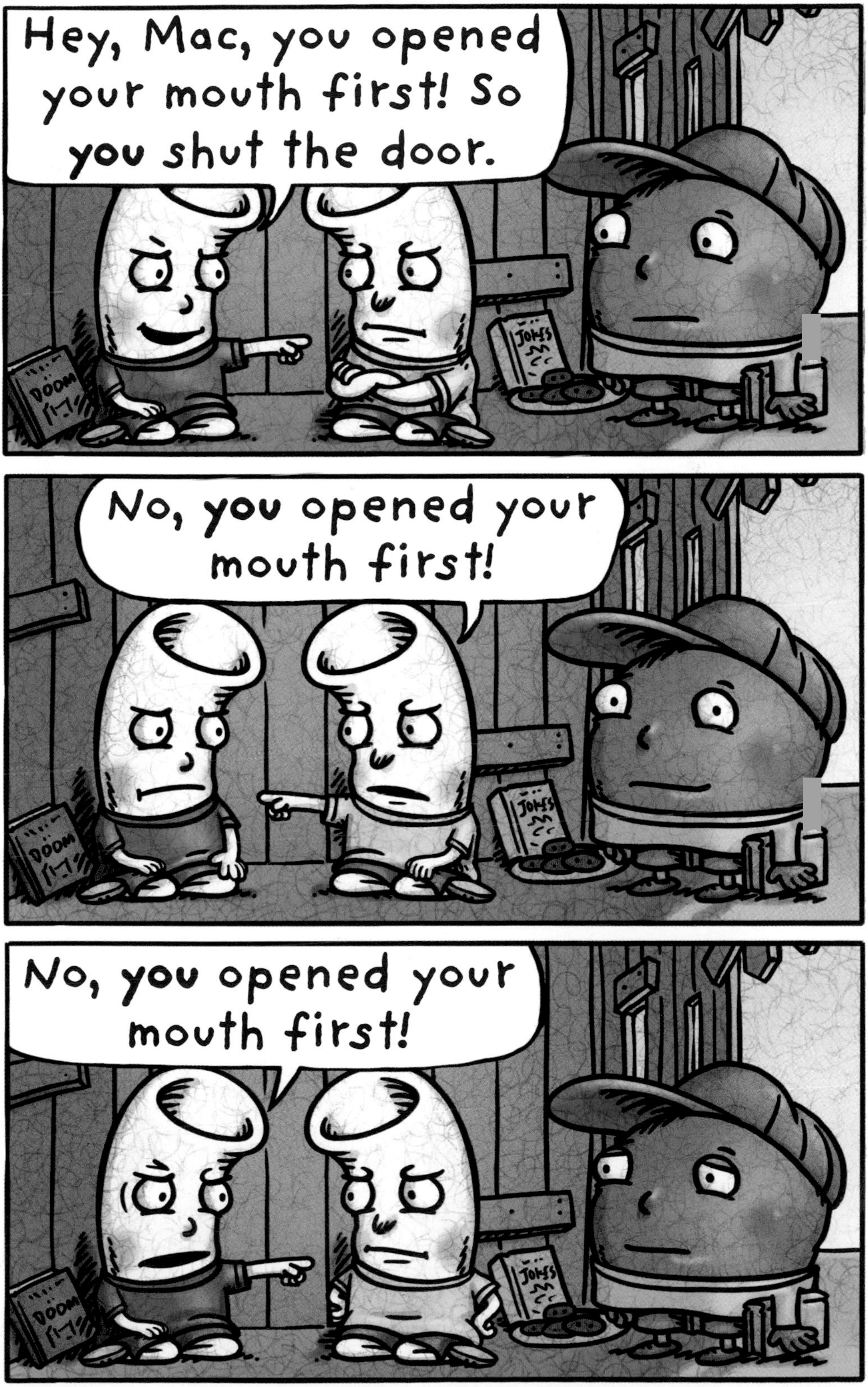
Hey, Mac, you opened your mouth first! So you shut the door.
DOOM
JOKES
No, you opened your mouth first!
DOOM
JOKES
No, you opened your mouth first!
DOOM
JOKES

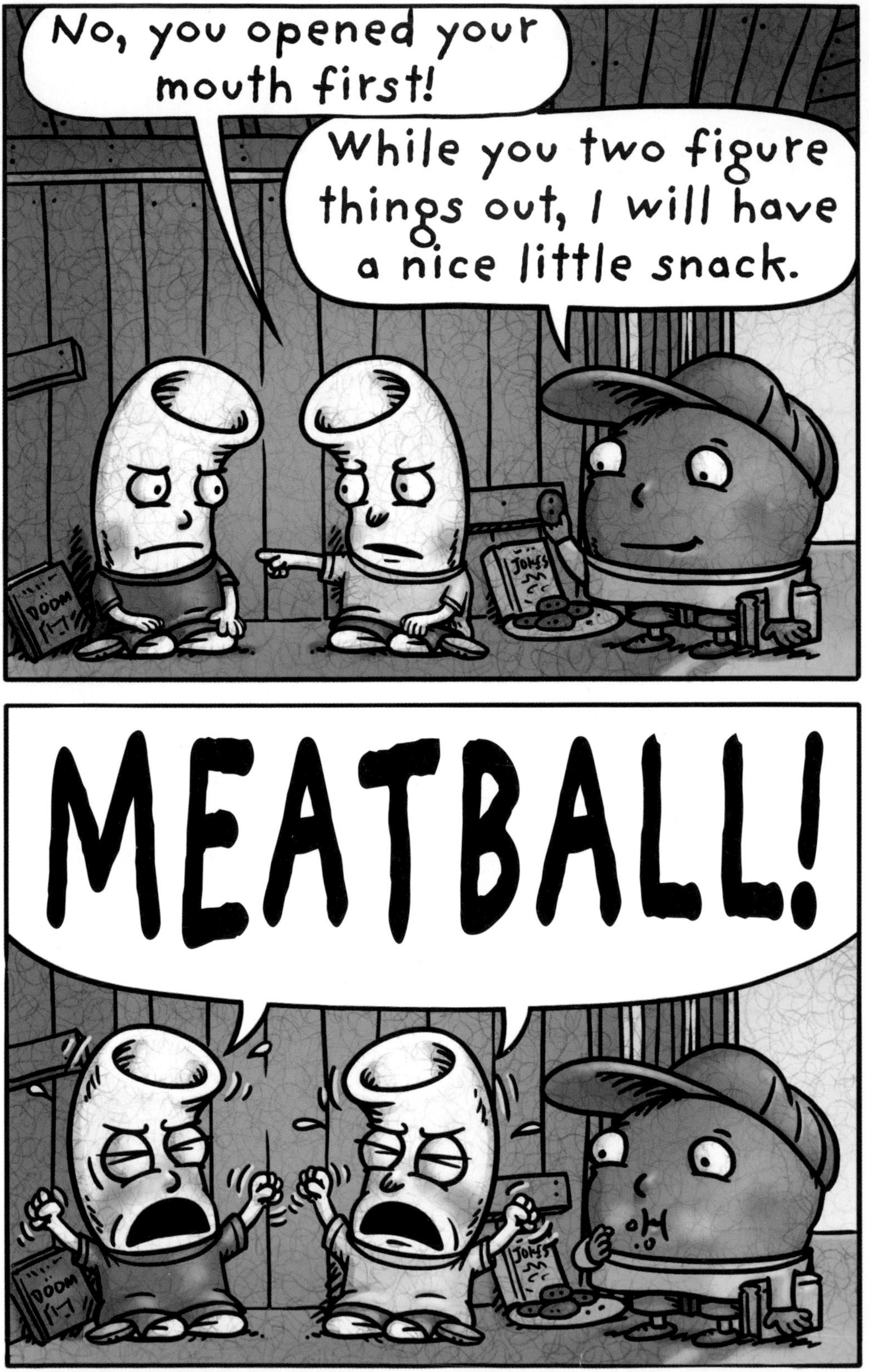
No, you opened your mouth first!
While you two figure things out, I will have a nice little snack.
MEATBALL!

CHAPTER 3

TAKING THE FORTRESS

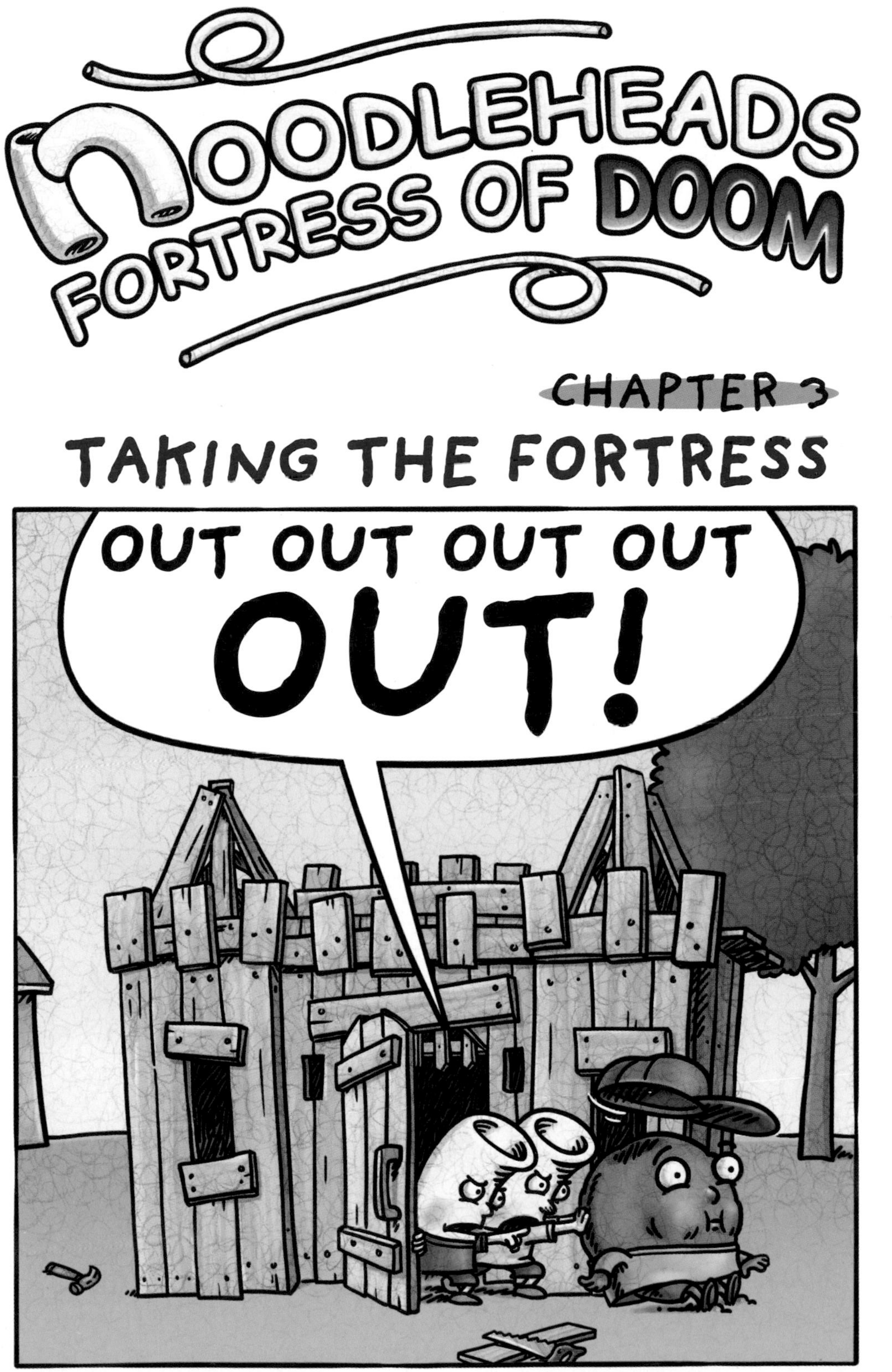
OUT OUT OUT OUT
OUT!

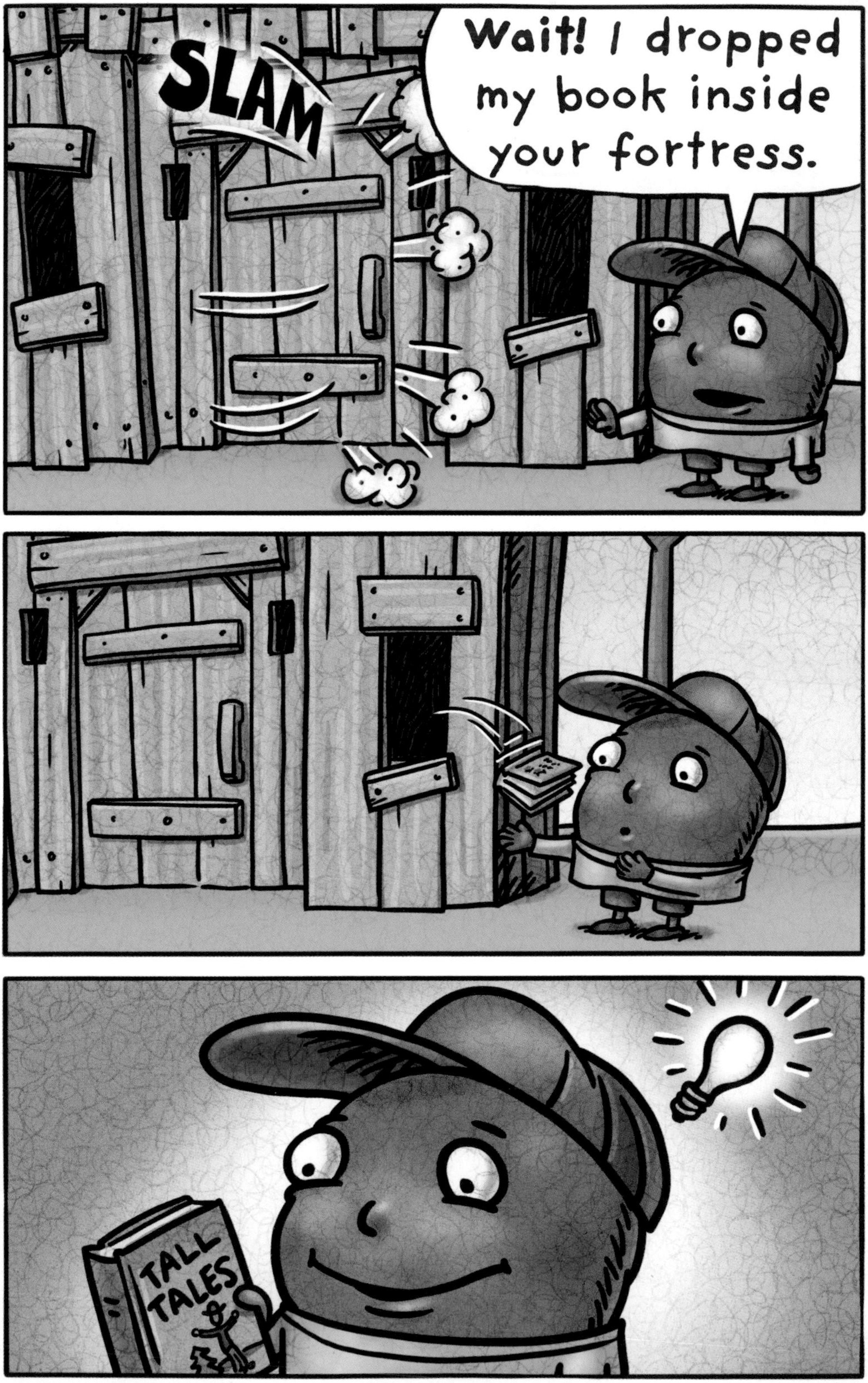
SLAM
Wait! I dropped my book inside your fortress.
TALL TALES

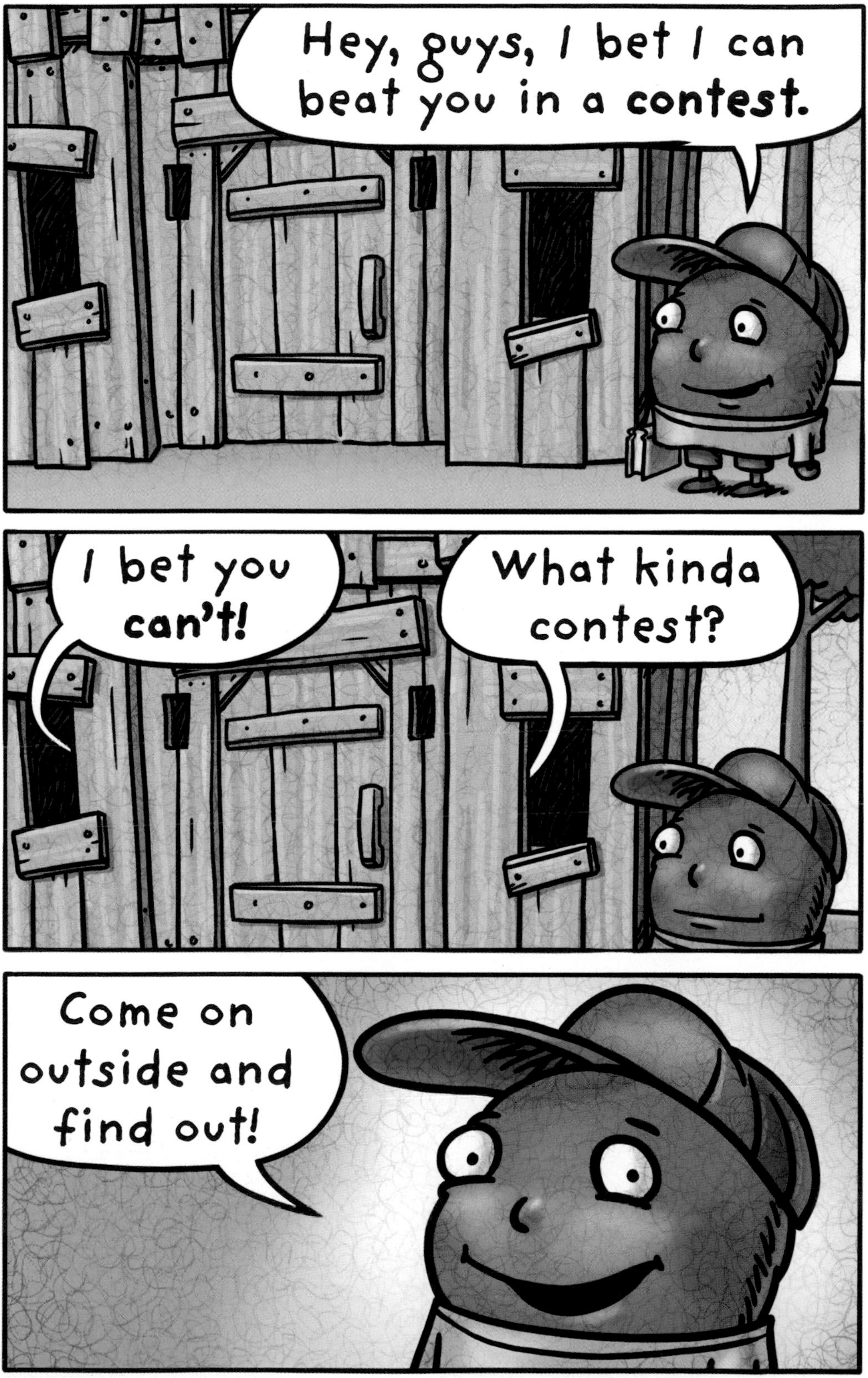
Hey, guys, I bet I can beat you in a **contest**.
I bet you **can't!**
What kinda contest?
Come on outside and find out!

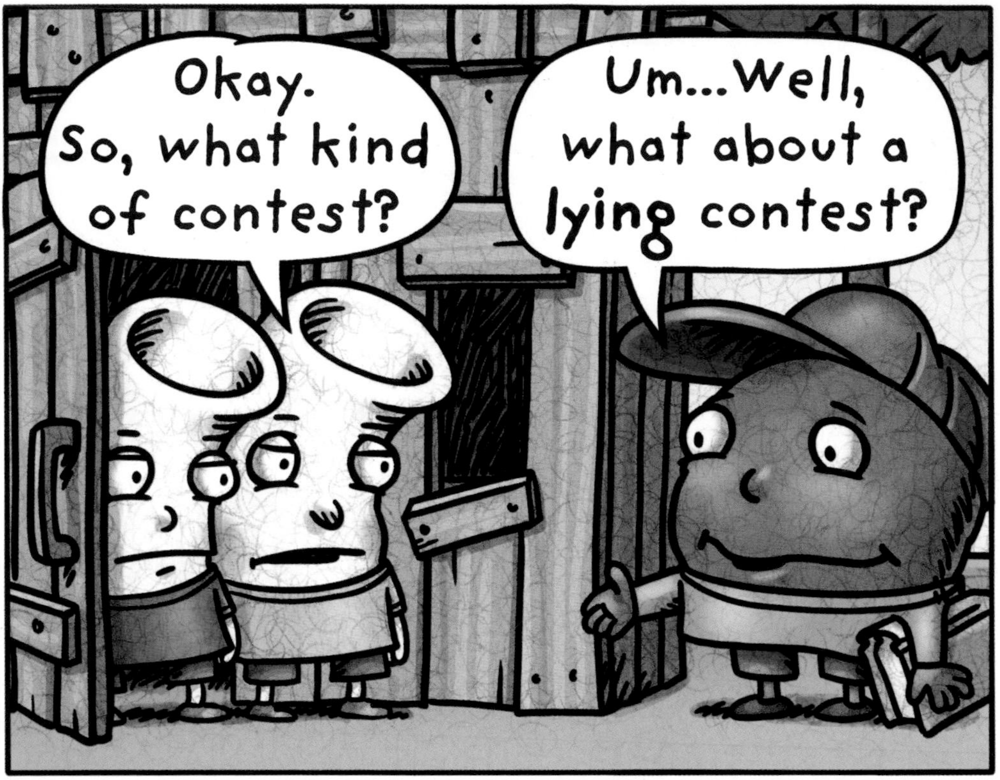
Okay. So, what kind of contest?
Um...Well, what about a lying contest?

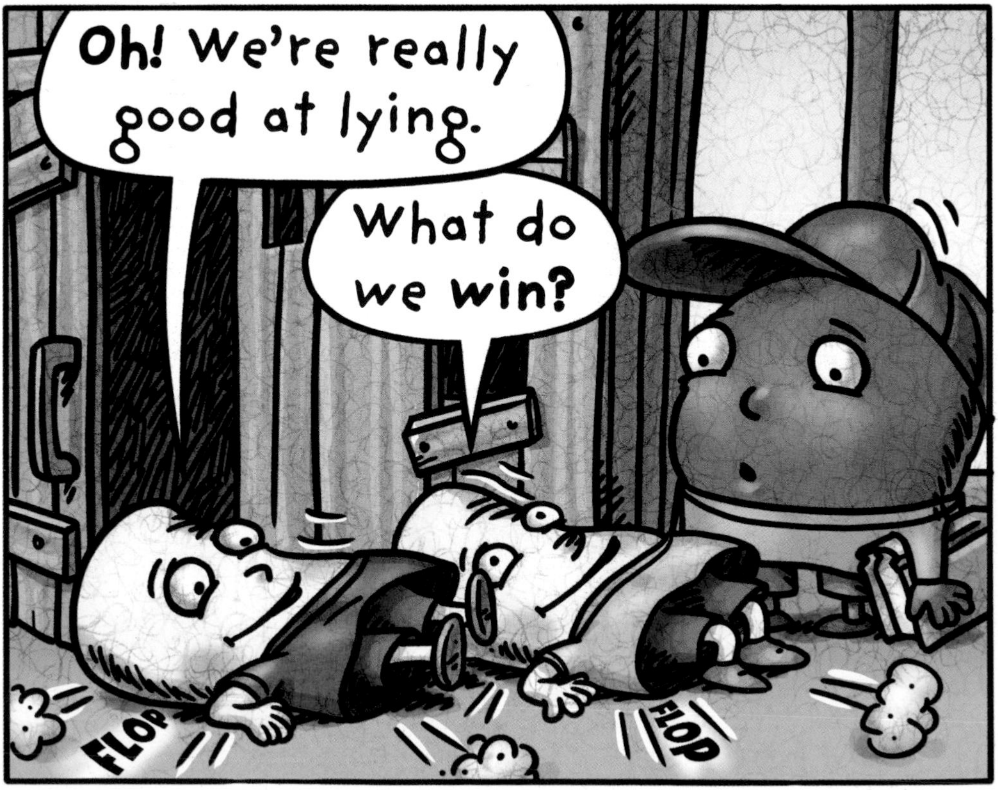
Oh! We're really good at lying.
What do we win?
FLOP
FLOP

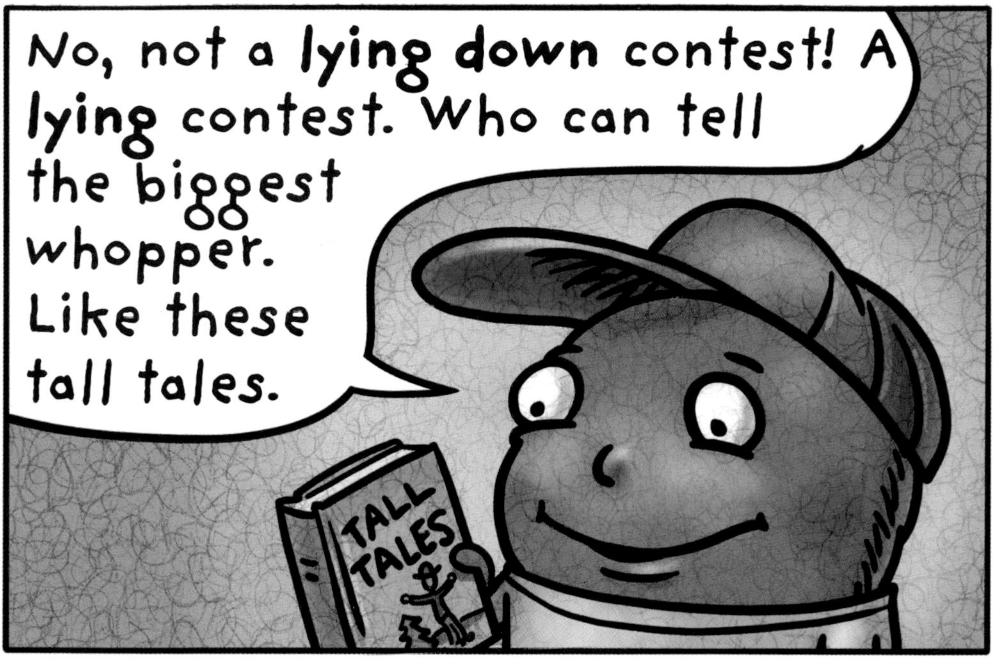
No, not a **lying down** contest! A **lying** contest. Who can tell the biggest whopper. Like these tall tales.
TALL TALES

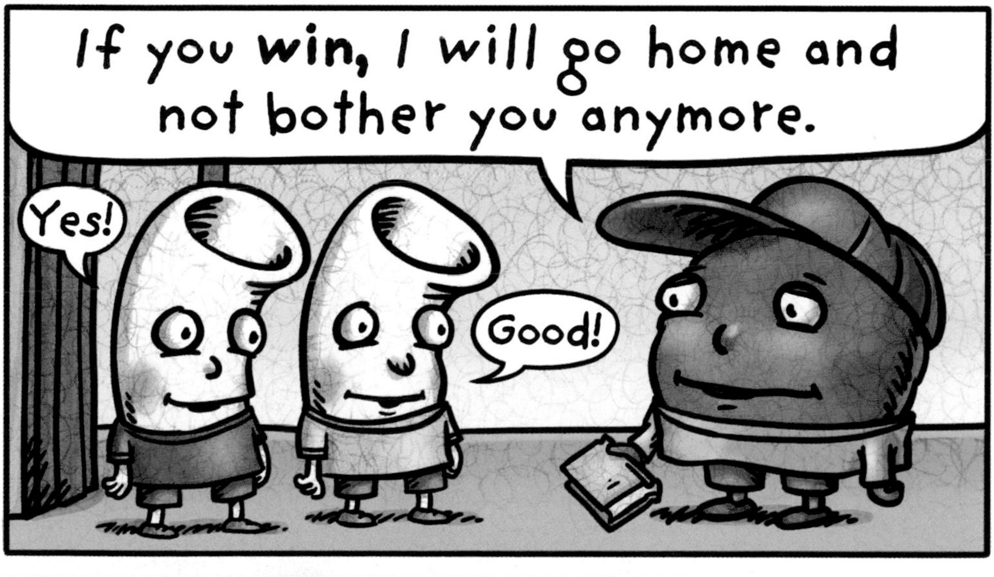
If you **win**, I will go home and not bother you anymore.
Yes!
Good!

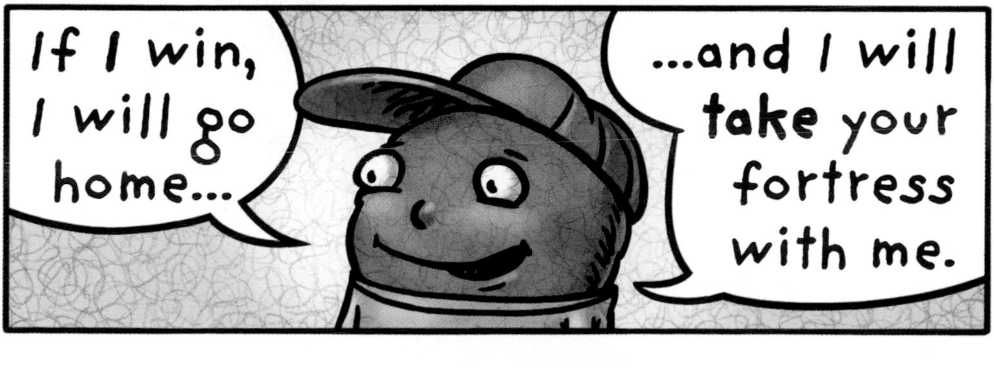
If I win, I will go home...
...and I will **take** your fortress with me.

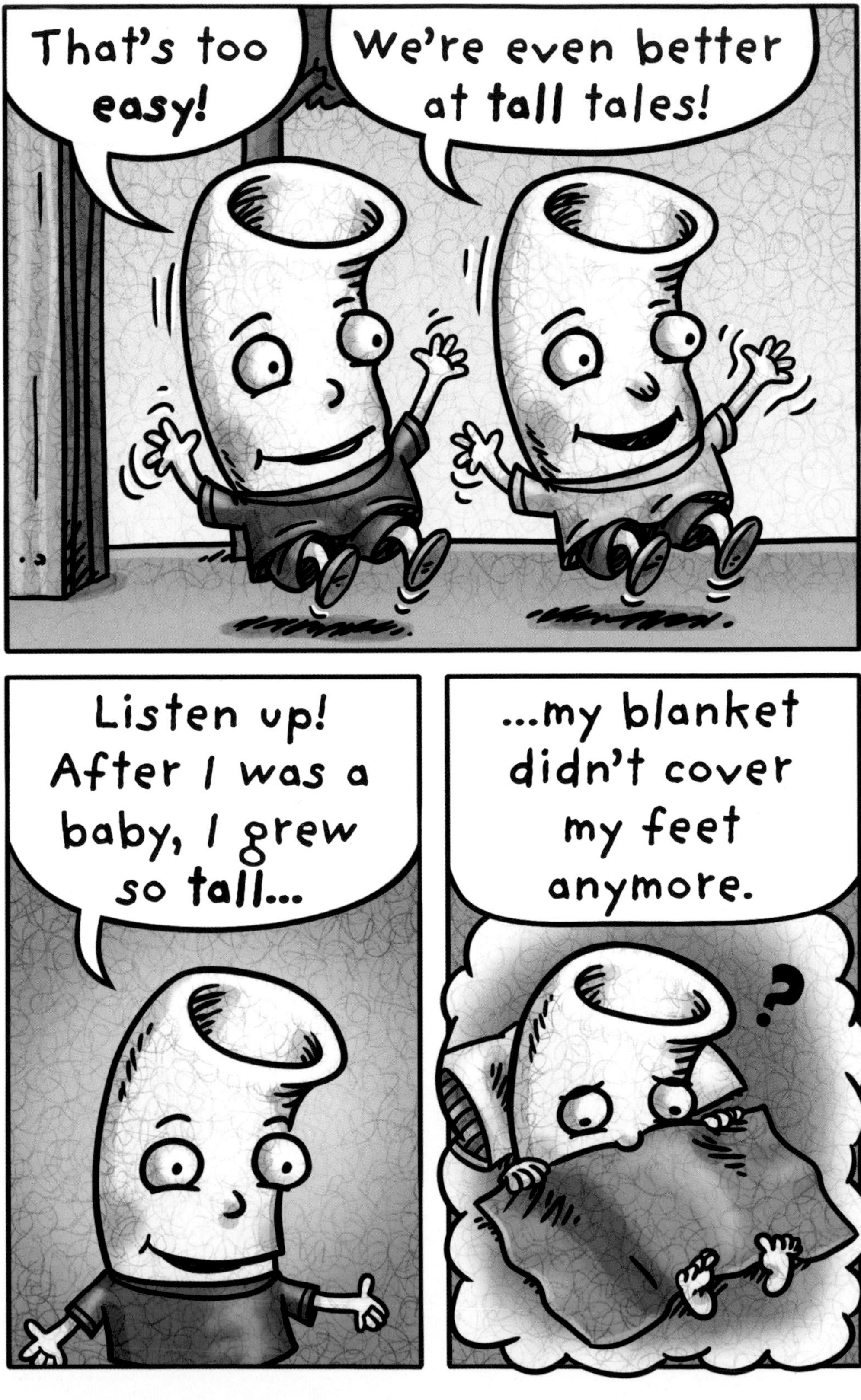
That's too easy!
We're even better at tall tales!
Listen up! After I was a baby, I grew so tall...
...my blanket didn't cover my feet anymore.
?

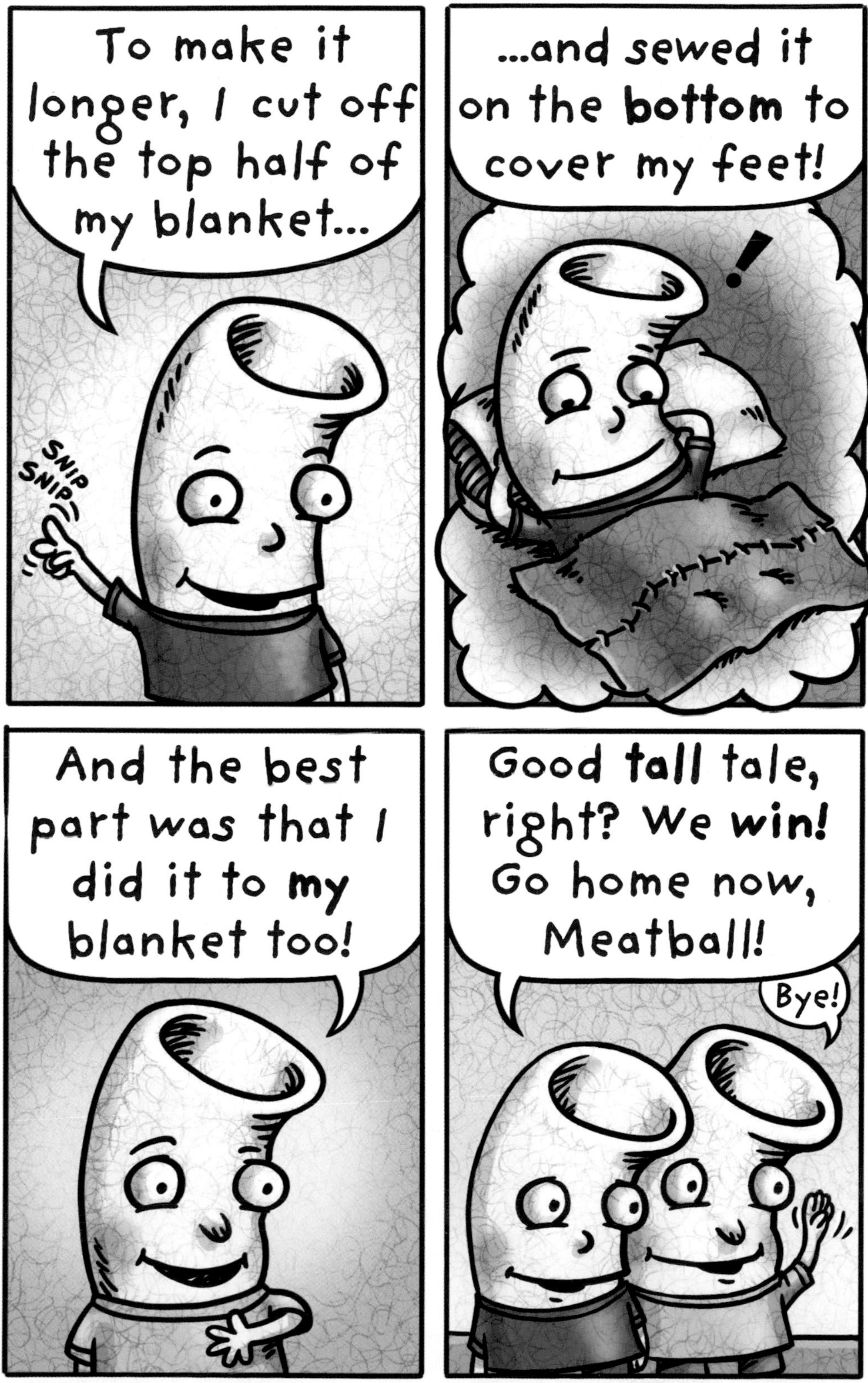
To make it longer, I cut off the top half of my blanket...
SNIP SNIP
...and sewed it on the bottom to cover my feet!
!
And the best part was that I did it to my blanket too!
Good tall tale, right? We win! Go home now, Meatball!
Bye!

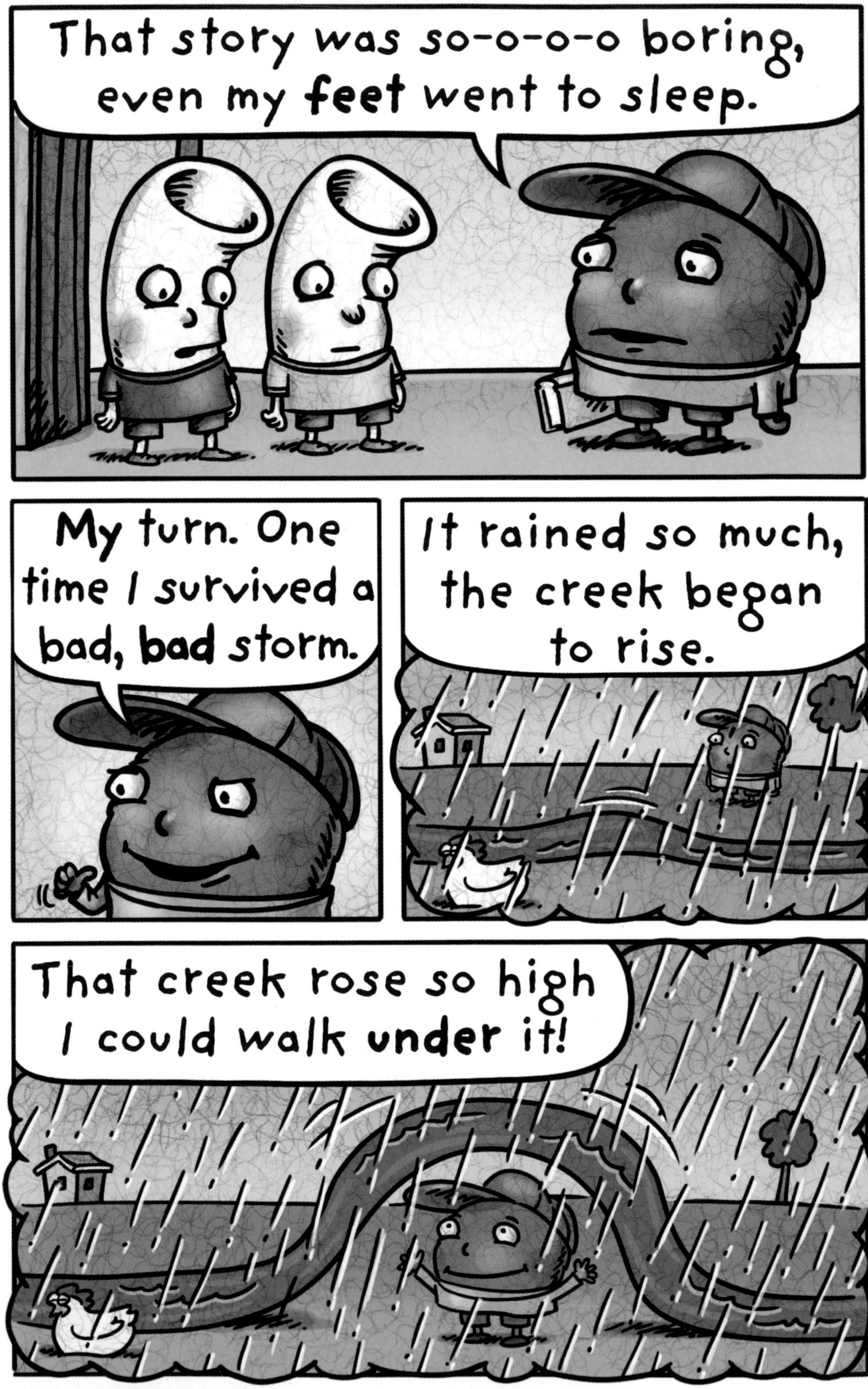
That story was so-o-o-o boring, even my feet went to sleep.
My turn. One time I survived a bad, bad storm.
It rained so much, the creek began to rise.
That creek rose so high I could walk under it!

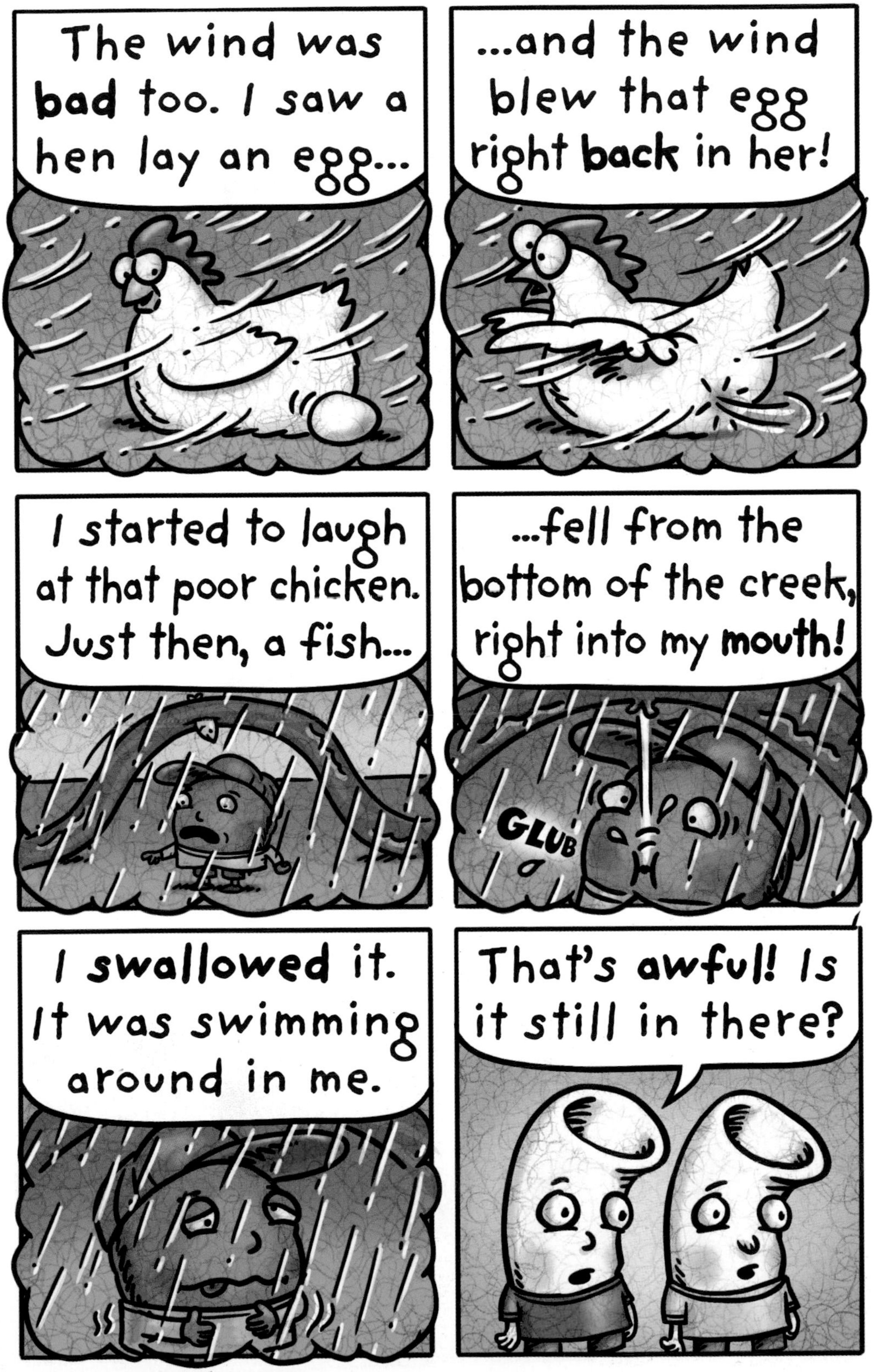
The wind was bad too. I saw a hen lay an egg...
...and the wind blew that egg right back in her!
I started to laugh at that poor chicken. Just then, a fish...
...fell from the bottom of the creek, right into my mouth!
GLUB
I swallowed it. It was swimming around in me.
That's awful! Is it still in there?

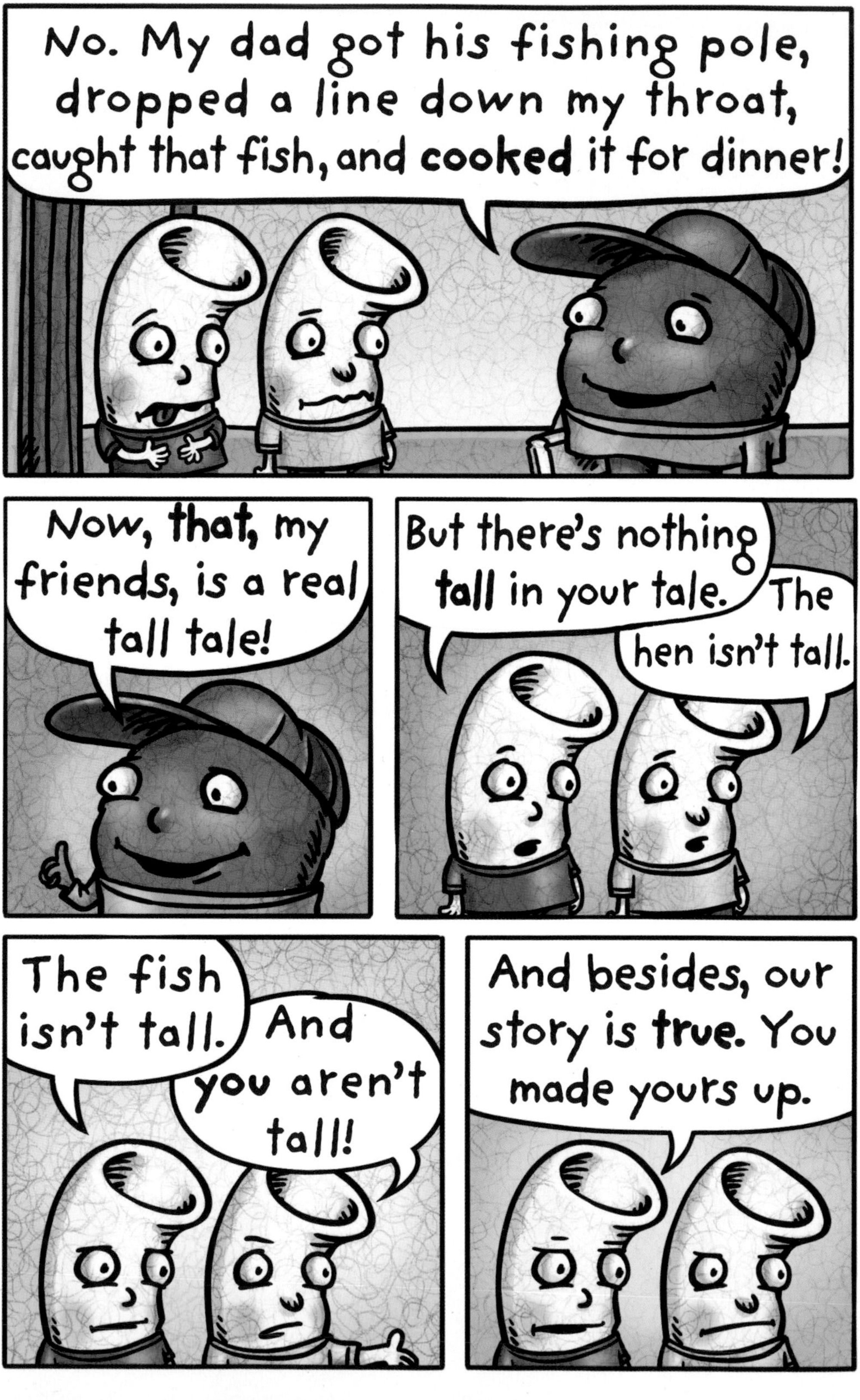
No. My dad got his fishing pole, dropped a line down my throat, caught that fish, and **cooked** it for dinner!
Now, **that**, my friends, is a real tall tale!
But there's nothing **tall** in your tale.
The hen isn't tall.
The fish isn't tall.
And you aren't tall!
And besides, our story is **true**. You made yours up.

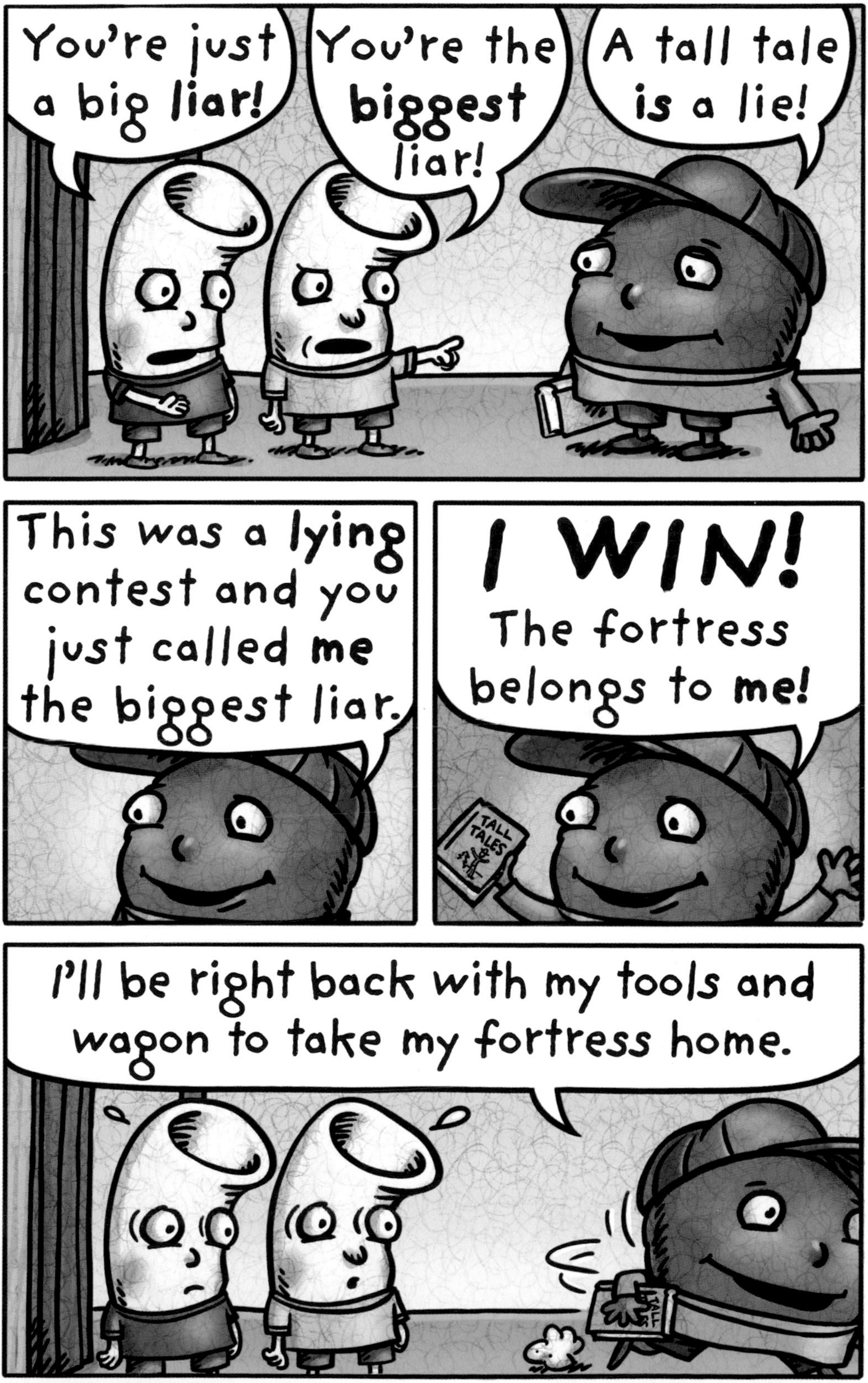
You're just a big liar!
You're the biggest liar!
A tall tale is a lie!
This was a lying contest and you just called me the biggest liar.
I WIN! The fortress belongs to me!
TALL TALES
I'll be right back with my tools and wagon to take my fortress home.

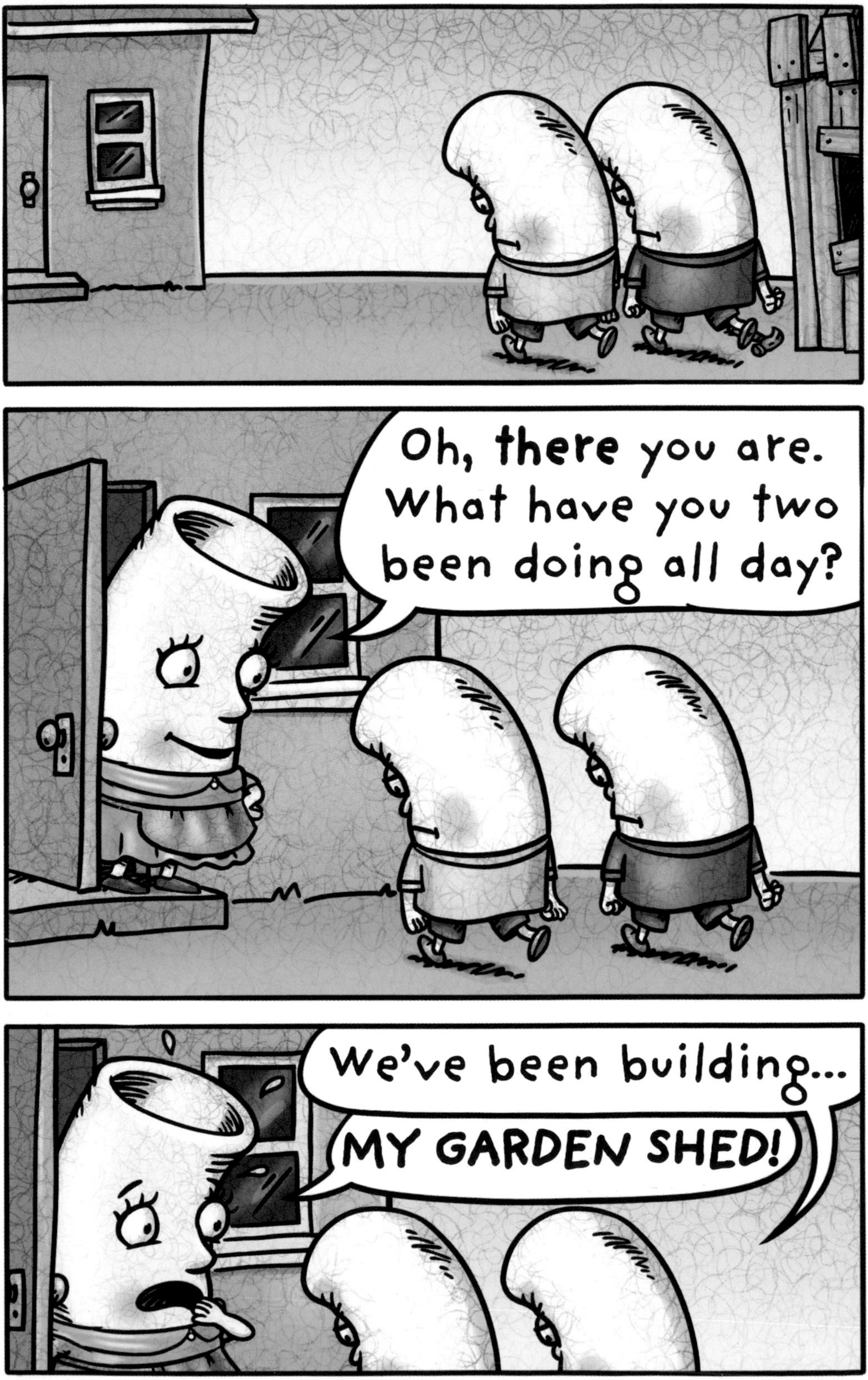
Oh, there you are. What have you two been doing all day?
We've been building...
MY GARDEN SHED!

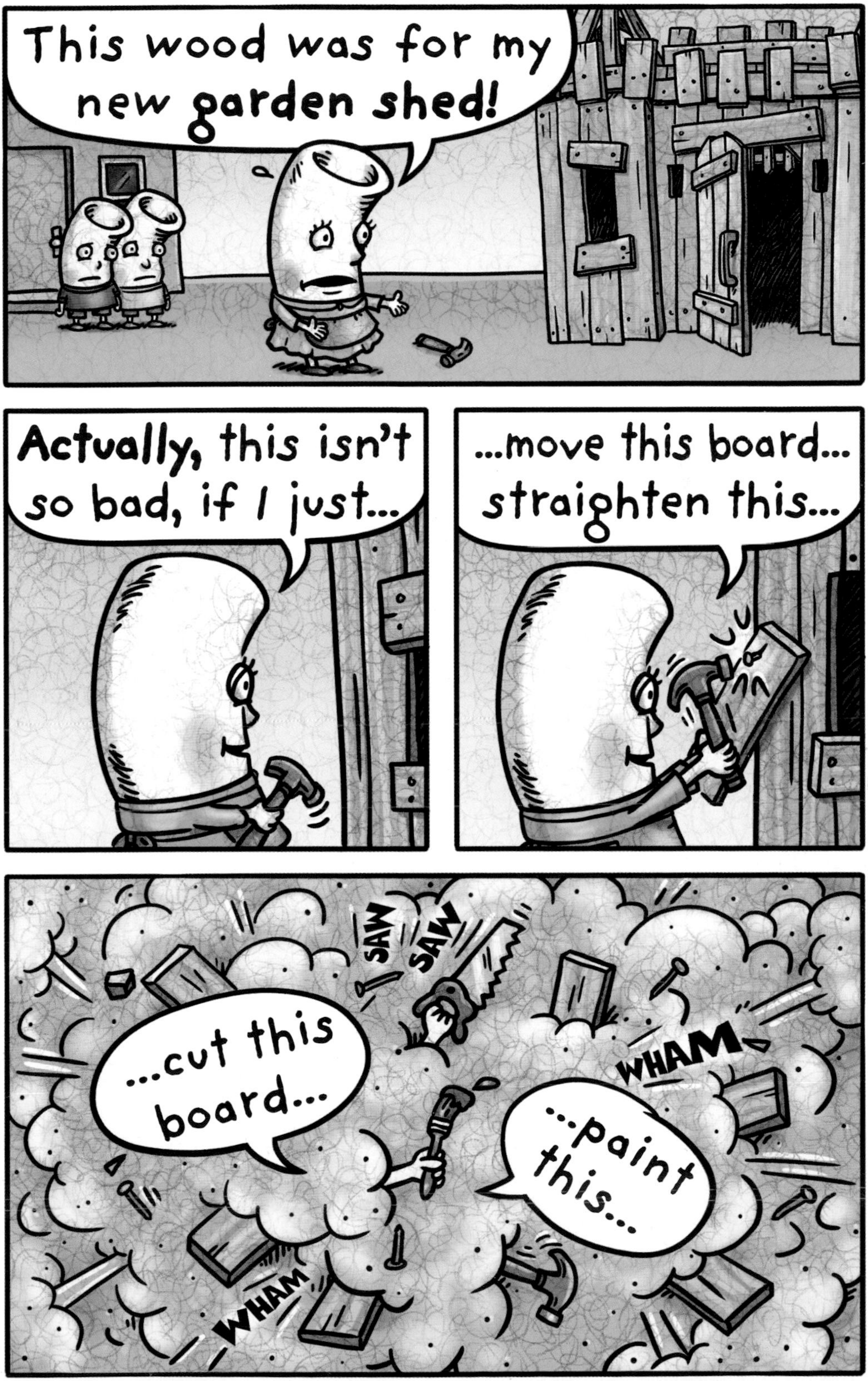

This wood was for my new garden shed!
Actually, this isn't so bad, if I just...
...move this board... straighten this...
SAW
SAW
...cut this board...
WHAM
...paint this...
WHAM

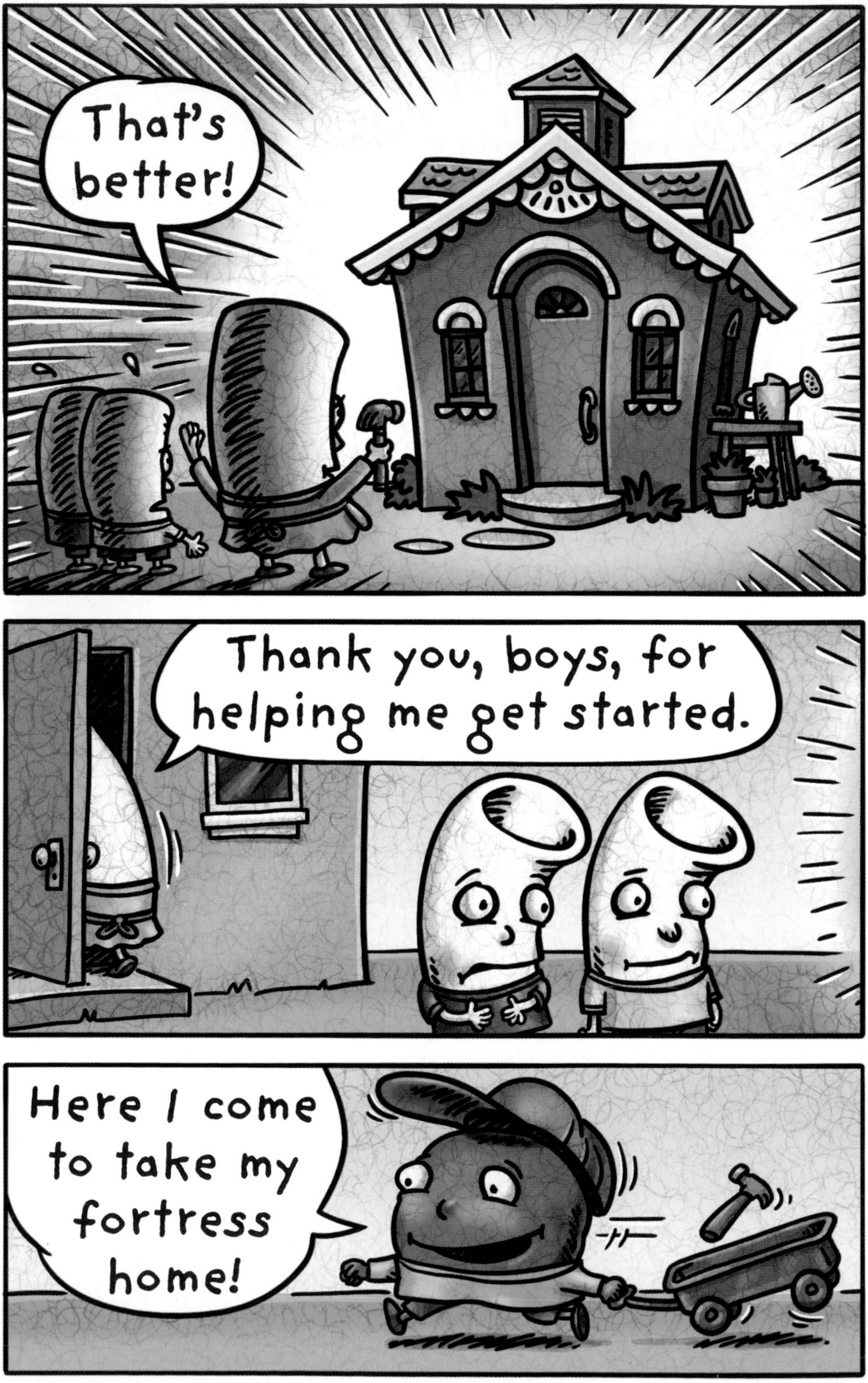
That's better!
Thank you, boys, for helping me get started.
Here I come to take my fortress home!

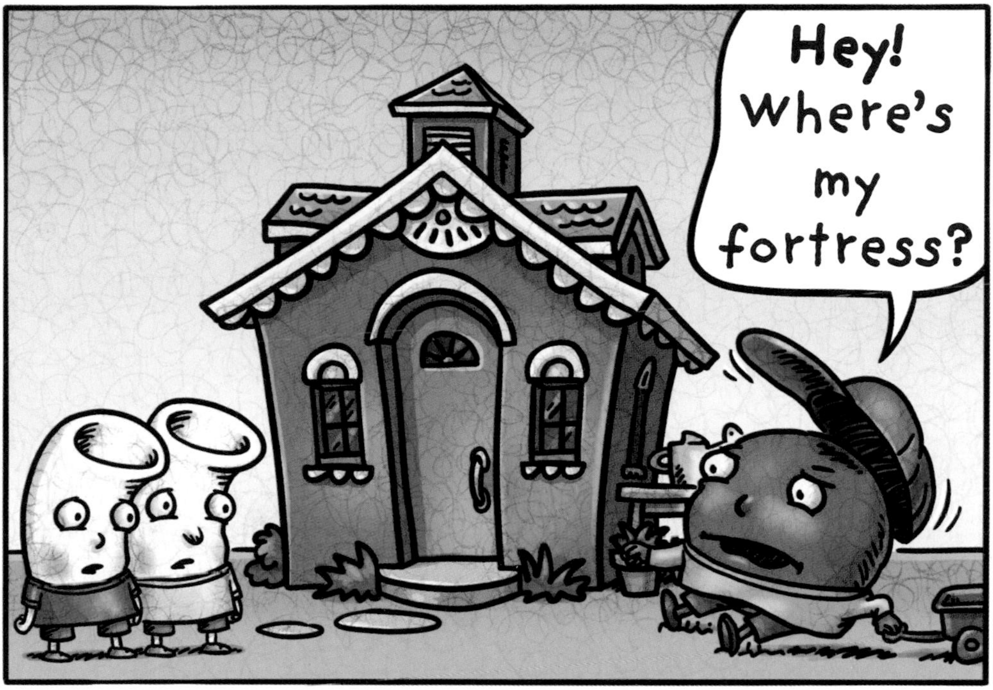
Hey! Where's my fortress?

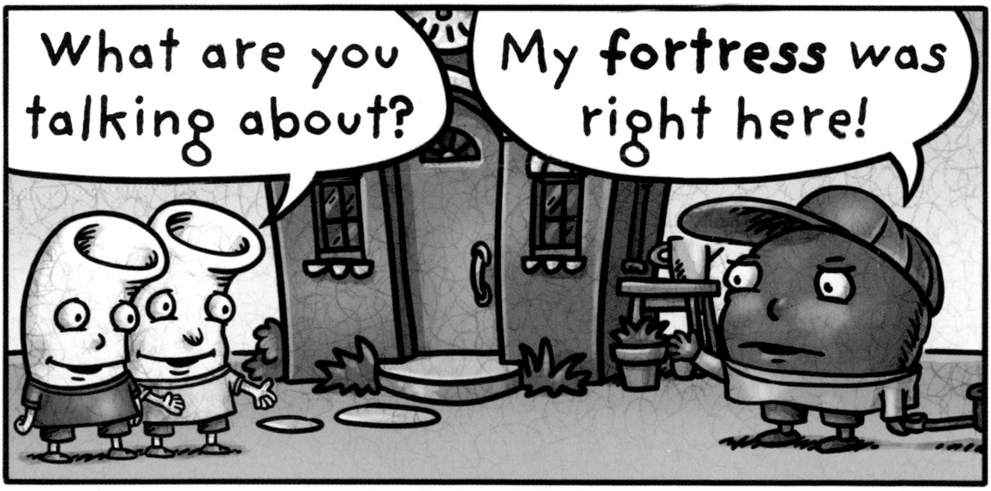
What are you talking about?
My **fortress** was right here!

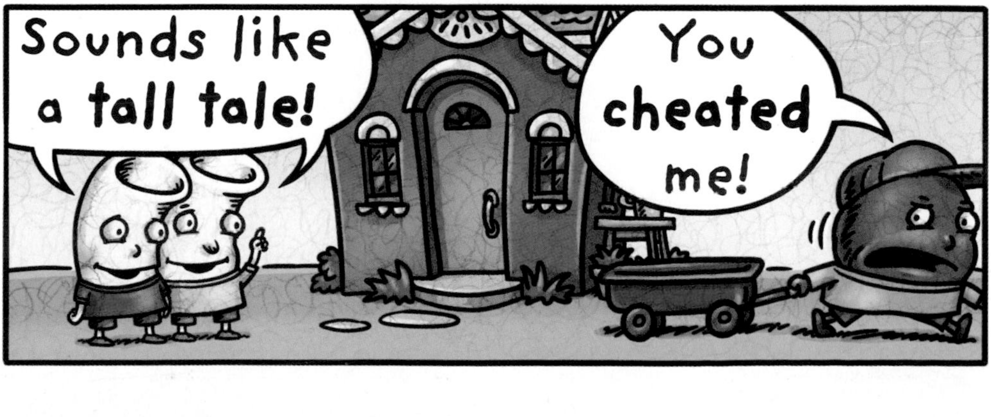
Sounds like a **tall tale**!
You **cheated** me!

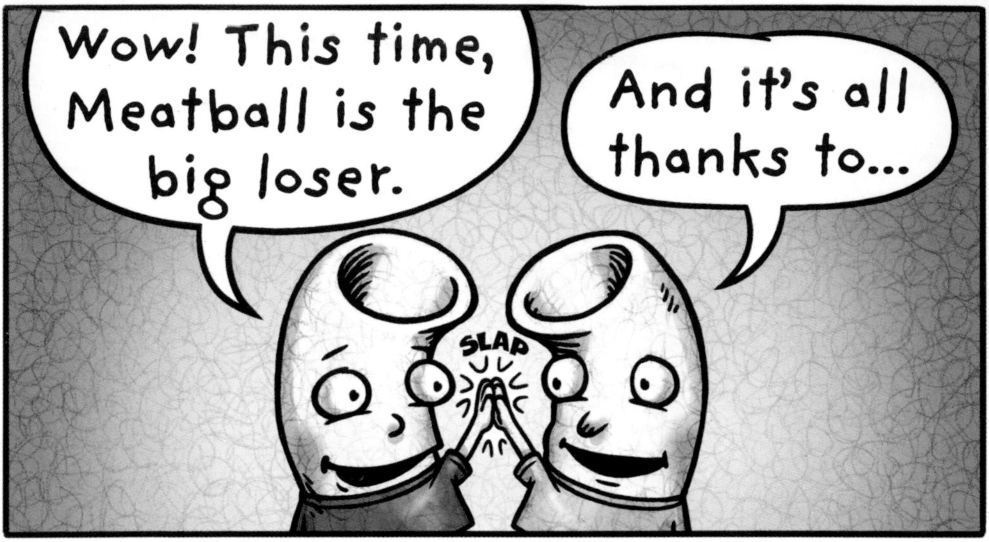
Wow! This time, Meatball is the big loser.
And it's all thanks to...
SLAP

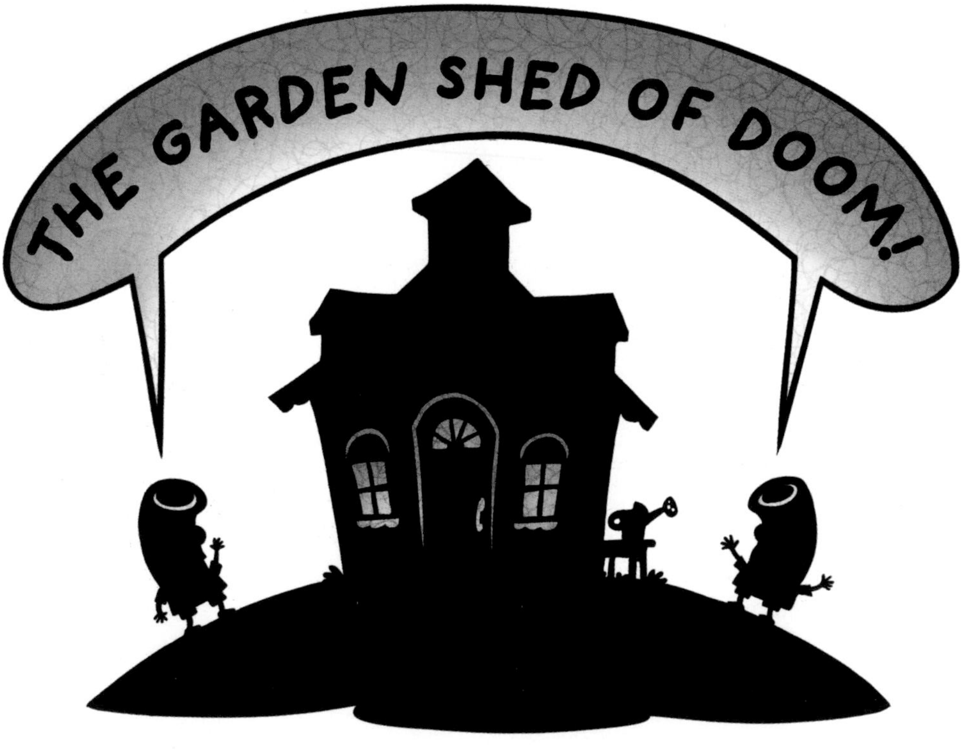
THE GARDEN SHED OF DOOM!

Authors' Notes

Story Sources for *Noodleheads Fortress of Doom*

Tales of fools, also called "noodles" or "noodleheads," have been told for as long as people have told stories. In 1888, W. A. Clouston wrote a scholarly book called *The Book of Noodles* in which he described numerous stories that had been told for hundreds of years, with quite a few dating back over two millennia. We have used these old stories as inspiration for Mac and Mac's adventures.

Everyone has done something foolish. Here is one of many stories that Mitch and Martha could tell. In 1999, they were nearing the end of a five-hour drive home when they heard a news report on the radio about Yo-Yo Ma having left his cello in a taxi in New York City. They suddenly remembered that their laptop was still in the principal's office at the school where they had worked that week; they had stored it there so it would not sit in their hot car. Noodleheads! It took a good amount of money to ship it home safely. The only thing that made them feel better was that one of their heroes had done something far more foolish—left his rare, treasured cello, which was worth millions of dollars, in the trunk of a cab. Fortunately, the cello was found before his evening concert and all was well—just as often happens in the old stories. In spite of their foolishness, things usually turn out fine in the end for noodleheads, perhaps because they are generally kind and well meaning. Children find comfort in the fact that a foolish mistake usually doesn't mean the end of the world. Even if Mac and Mac don't learn from their mistakes, children who read about their adventures do. Noodlehead stories also help them understand humor, logical thinking, and the importance of distinguishing between what's true and what's a lie. Children quickly see that they should not always believe what they hear, especially when the source is a bully like Meatball.

The motifs to which we refer in the information that follows are from *The Storyteller's Sourcebook: A Subject, Title, and Motif Index to Folklore Collections for Children* by Margaret Read MacDonald, first edition, (Detroit: Gale, 1982) and second edition by Margaret Read MacDonald and Brian W. Sturm (Detroit: Gale, 2001). Tale types are from *A Guide to Folktales in the English Language* by D. L. Ashliman (NY: Greenwood, 1987).

Chapter 1: If We Build It . . .

Jokes are a genre of folklore—the stories, beliefs, customs, and traditions of a culture or community of people that are passed along by word of mouth. Although it's possible that the idea of knock-knock jokes dates back to Shakespeare, this joke form became popular among adults in the 1930s in the United States. Although their popularity has waxed and waned, knock-knock jokes are still popular today, but are primarily thought of as jokes for children.

Chapter 2: Guarding the Door

Inspiration for this chapter came from tale type 1009, *Guarding the Door by Carrying It Away,* which is known throughout Europe and the Middle East. A retelling by Martha and Mitch, "When Giufa Guarded the Goldsmith's Door," can be found in *Noodlehead Stories: World Tales Kids Can Read & Tell* (Atlanta: August House Publishers, 2000). Sources for that retelling included Clouston's *The Book of Noodles* and *Italian Folktales* by Italo Calvino (New York: Harcourt Brace, 1980). Another inspiration was "Who Will Close the Door?" which can be found in Martha and Mitch's book *Stories in My Pocket: Tales Kids Can Tell* (Golden, CO: Fulcrum Publishing, 1996). The tale type is 1351, *Silence Wager,* and the motif is J2511.0.3 *First to speak must close door.* The story originated in India and was eventually well known throughout Europe; a famous version is the Scottish ballad "Get Up and Bar the Door."

Chapter 3: Taking the Fortress

Tall tales—stories that are outrageous exaggerations or outright lies told as if they are true—have a long history. Meatball understands that the teller of tall tales lies for the fun of it, uses creativity and invention to make others laugh, and does not expect to be believed. Because people have a natural tendency to compete with or "one-up" one another when telling these stories, lying contests and Liars' Clubs were born. Even today, there are several official Liars' Contests still held throughout the world. The story about the creek rising and the wind blowing the egg back into the hen was inspired by the story "Rain and Mud" by the late Chuck Larkin, a master teller of tall tales. It can be found at www.chucklarkin.com/stories/Short_Tales.pdf. Both stories fit into the motif X1600 *Lies about weather and climate.* Mac and Mac's "brilliant" idea to cut off the bottom half of the blanket and sew it to the top in order to make it longer (J1978 *Quilt too short . . .*) falls under the broader category *Absurd Disregard of Facts.*

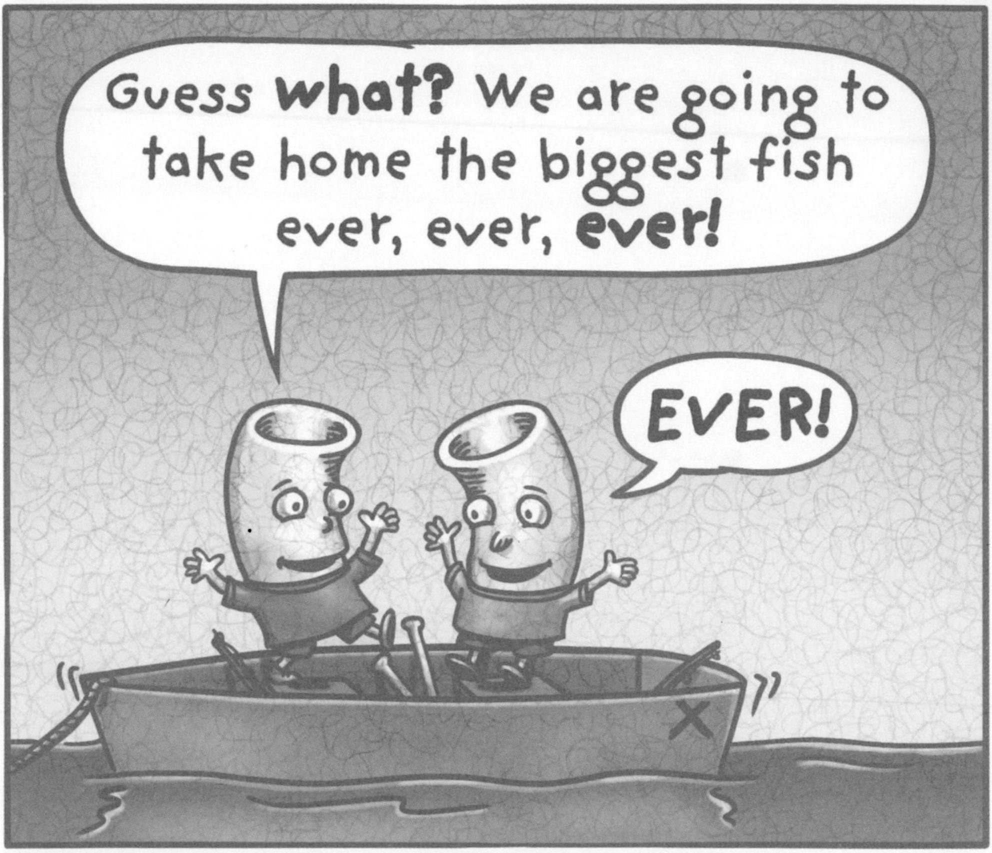
Guess what? We are going to take home the biggest fish ever, ever, ever!
EVER!

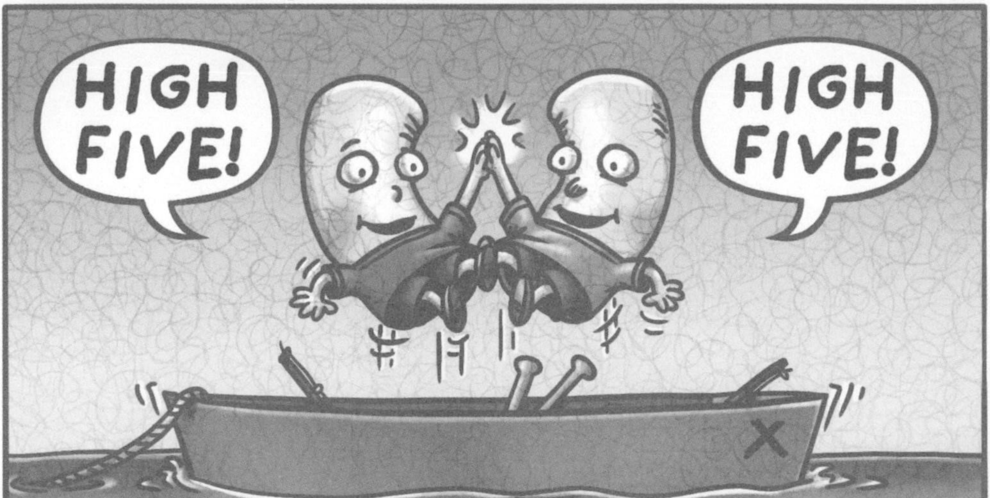
HIGH FIVE!
HIGH FIVE!